MINECRAFT™

STORIES FROM THE OVERWORLD

D0011750

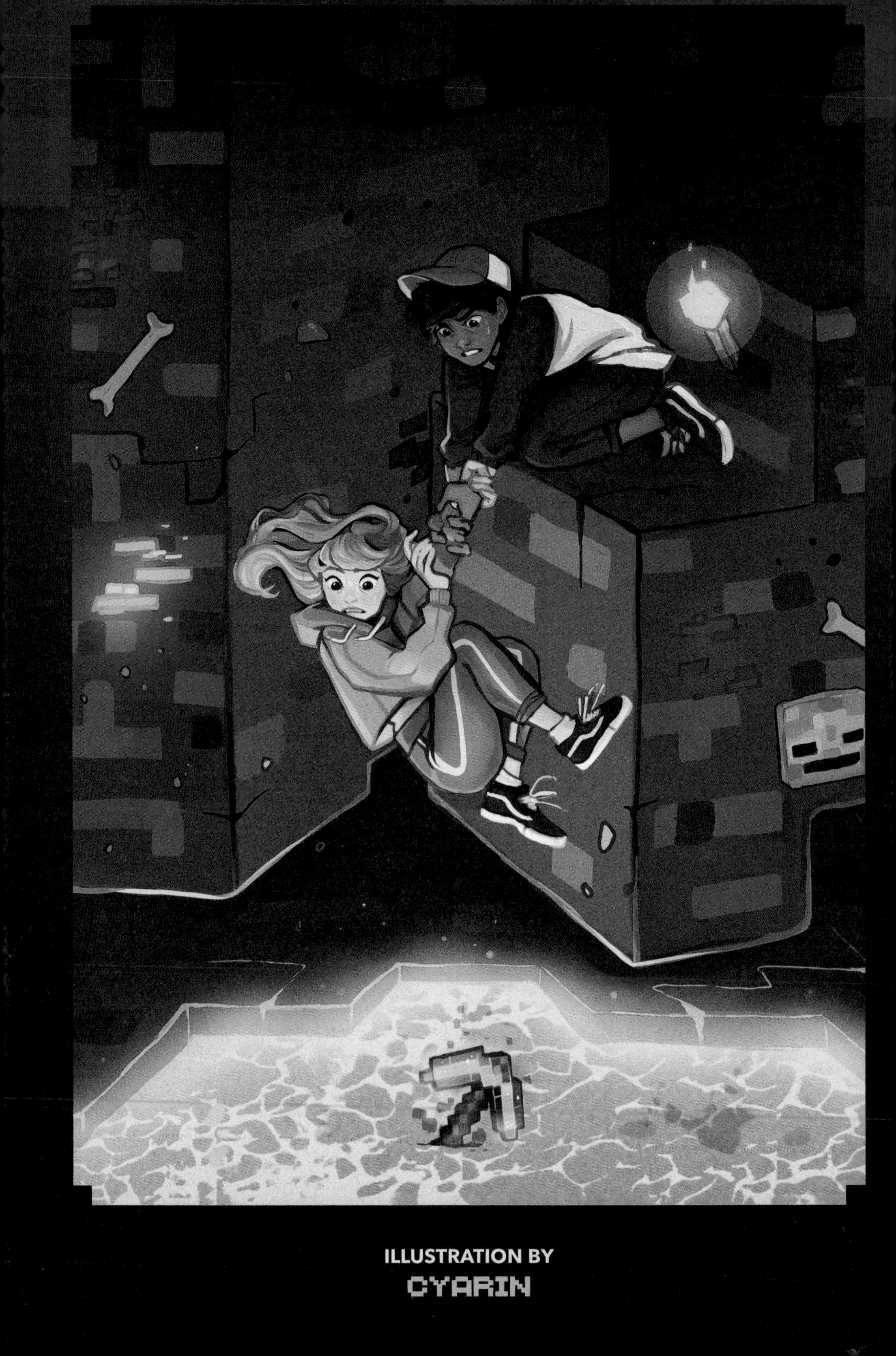

ILLUSTRATION BY
CYARIN

MINECRAFT

STORIES FROM THE OVERWORLD

PRESIDENT & PUBLISHER
MIKE RICHARDSON

EDITOR
SHANTEL LaROCQUE

ASSISTANT EDITOR
BRETT ISRAEL

DESIGNER
KEITH WOOD

DIGITAL ART TECHNICIAN
JOSIE CHRISTENSEN

SPECIAL THANKS TO
JENNIFER HAMMERVALD
AND ALEX WILTSHIRE

Published by Dark Horse Books
A division of Dark Horse Comics LLC
10956 SE Main Street
Milwaukie, OR 97222

To find a comics shop in your area, visit
ComicShopLocator.com.

First edition: October 2022
Scholastic Book Fairs and Clubs US Edition
ISBN 978-1-50673-405-7

10 9 8 7 6 5 4 3 2 1

Printed in Beauceville, Canada

MINECRAFT™
STORIES FROM THE OVERWORLD

Minecraft™ © 2019, 2021 Mojang AB. All Rights
Reserved. Minecraft, the Minecraft logo and the
Mojang Studios logo are trademarks of the Microsoft
group of companies. Dark Horse Books® and the
Dark Horse logo are registered trademarks of Dark
Horse Comics LLC. All rights reserved. No portion of
this publication may be reproduced or transmitted,
in any form or by any means, without the express
written permission of Dark Horse Comics LLC. Names,
characters, places, and incidents featured in this
publication either are the product of the author's
imagination or are used fictitiously. Any resemblance
to actual persons (living or dead), events, institu-
tions, or locales, without satiric intent, is coincidental.

Library of Congress Cataloging-in-Publication Data

Title: Minecraft : stories from the overworld.
Description: First edition. | Milwaukie, OR : Dark Horse Books, 2019.
Identifiers: LCCN 2019016371 | ISBN 9781506708331 (hardback)
Subjects: | BISAC: GAMES / Video & Electronic. | COMICS & GRAPHIC NOVELS /
   Media Tie-In.
Classification: LCC PZ7.7 .M555 2019 | DDC 741.5/973--dc23
LC record available at https://lccn.loc.gov/2019016371

MINECRAFT™

STORIES FROM THE OVERWORLD

NEIL HANKERSON
Executive Vice President

TOM WEDDLE
Chief Financial Officer

RANDY STRADLEY
Vice President of Publishing

NICK McWHORTER
Chief Business Development Officer

DALE LaFOUNTAIN
Chief Information Officer

MATT PARKINSON
Vice President of Marketing

CARA NIECE
Vice President of Production and Scheduling

MARK BERNARDI
Vice President of Book Trade and Digital Sales

KEN LIZZI
General Counsel

DAVE MARSHALL
Editor in Chief

DAVEY ESTRADA
Editorial Director

CHRIS WARNER
Senior Books Editor

CARY GRAZZINI
Director of Specialty Projects

LIA RIBACCHI
Art Director

VANESSA TODD-HOLMES
Director of Print Purchasing

MATT DRYER
Director of Digital Art and Prepress

MICHAEL GOMBOS
Senior Director of Licensed Publications

KARI YADRO
Director of Custom Programs

KARI TORSON
Director of International Licensing

SEAN BRICE
Director of Trade Sales

MINECRAFT.NET
DARKHORSE.COM

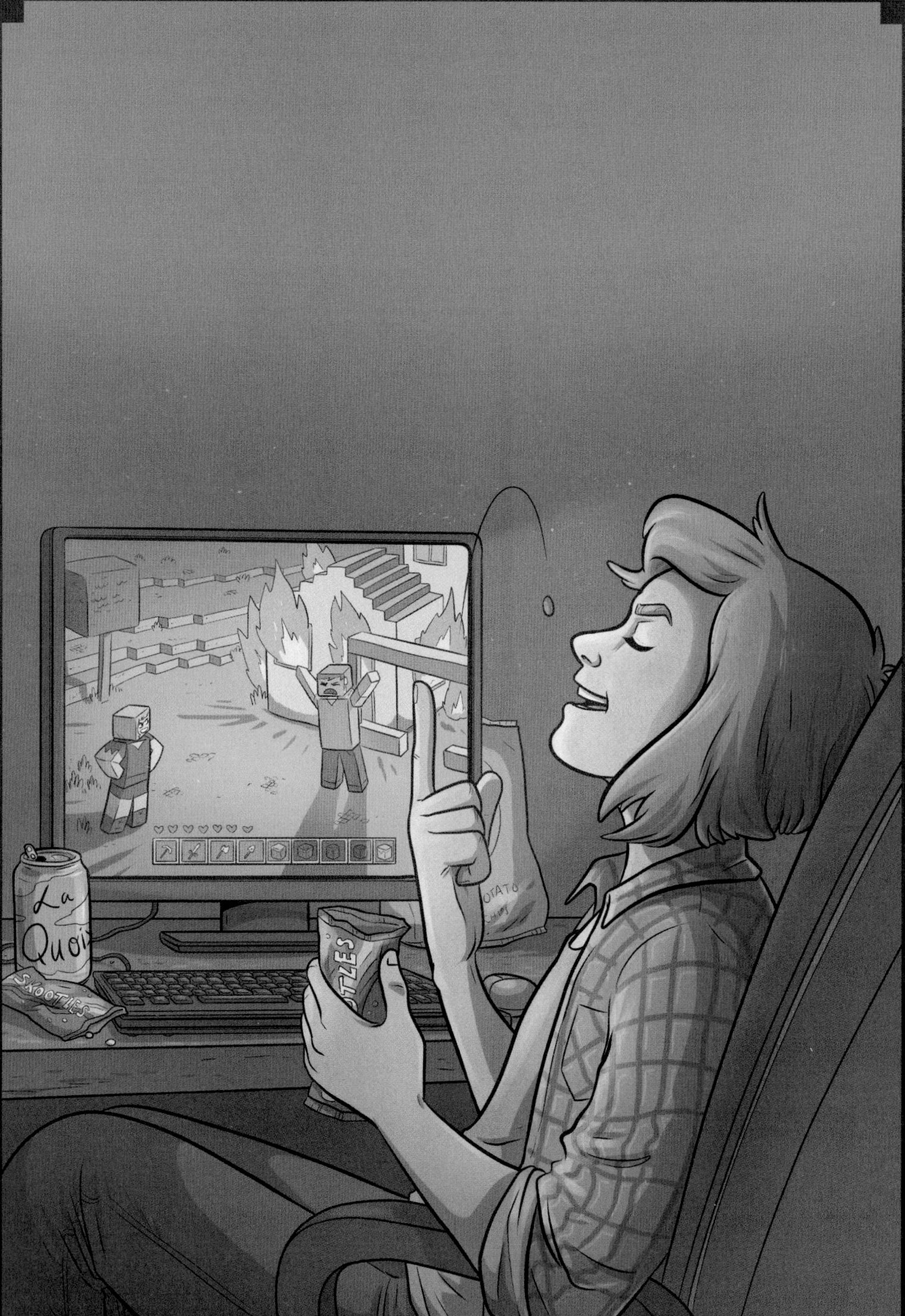
La
SKOOTIES

ILLUSTRATION BY
CASSIE ANDERSON

GRIEFER

STORY BY
HOPE LARSON

ART AND LETTERING BY
MEREDITH GRAN

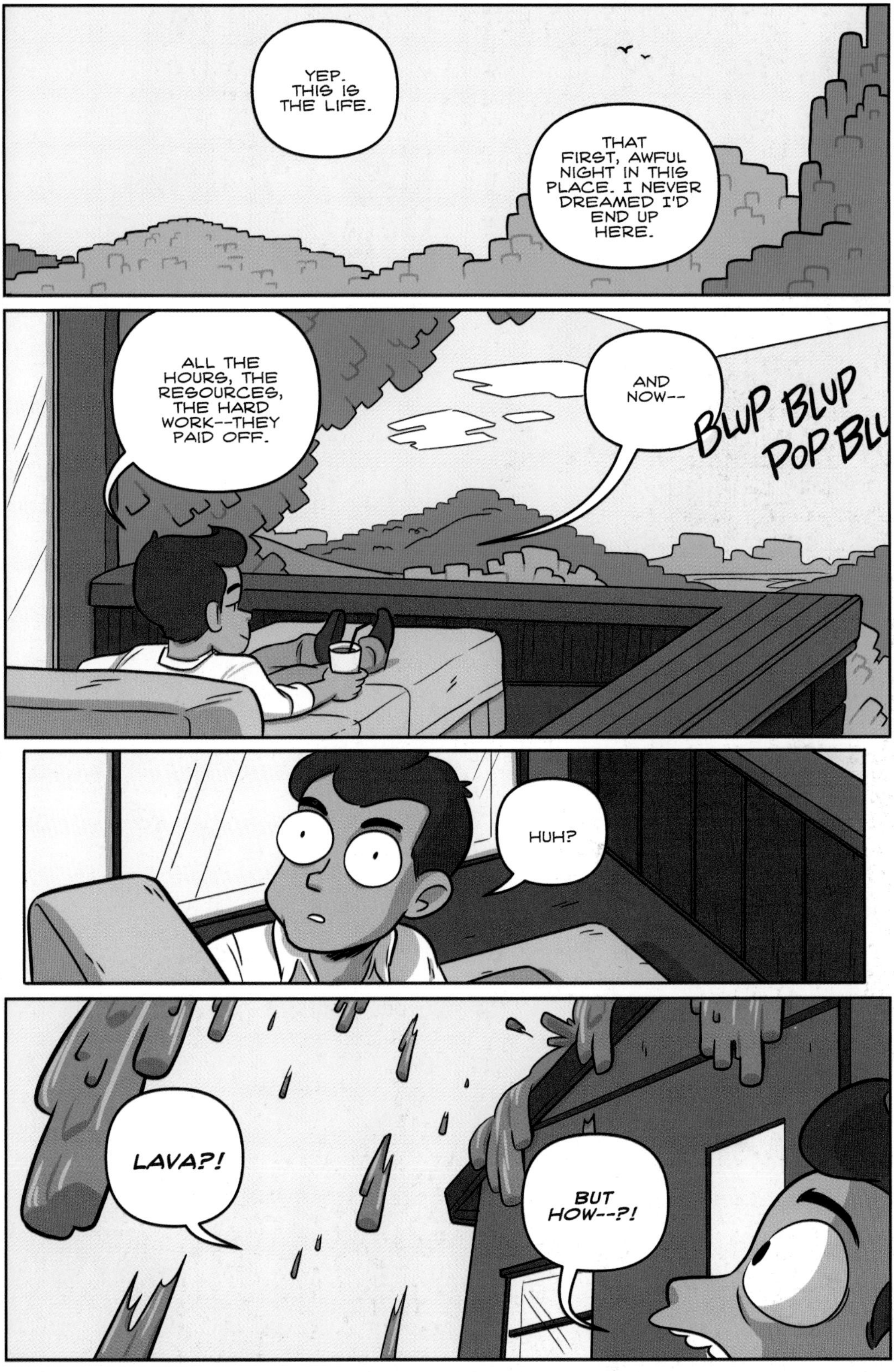
YEP. THIS IS THE LIFE.
THAT FIRST, AWFUL NIGHT IN THIS PLACE. I NEVER DREAMED I'D END UP HERE.
ALL THE HOURS, THE RESOURCES, THE HARD WORK--THEY PAID OFF.
AND NOW--
BLUP BLUP
HUH?
LAVA?!
BUT HOW--?!

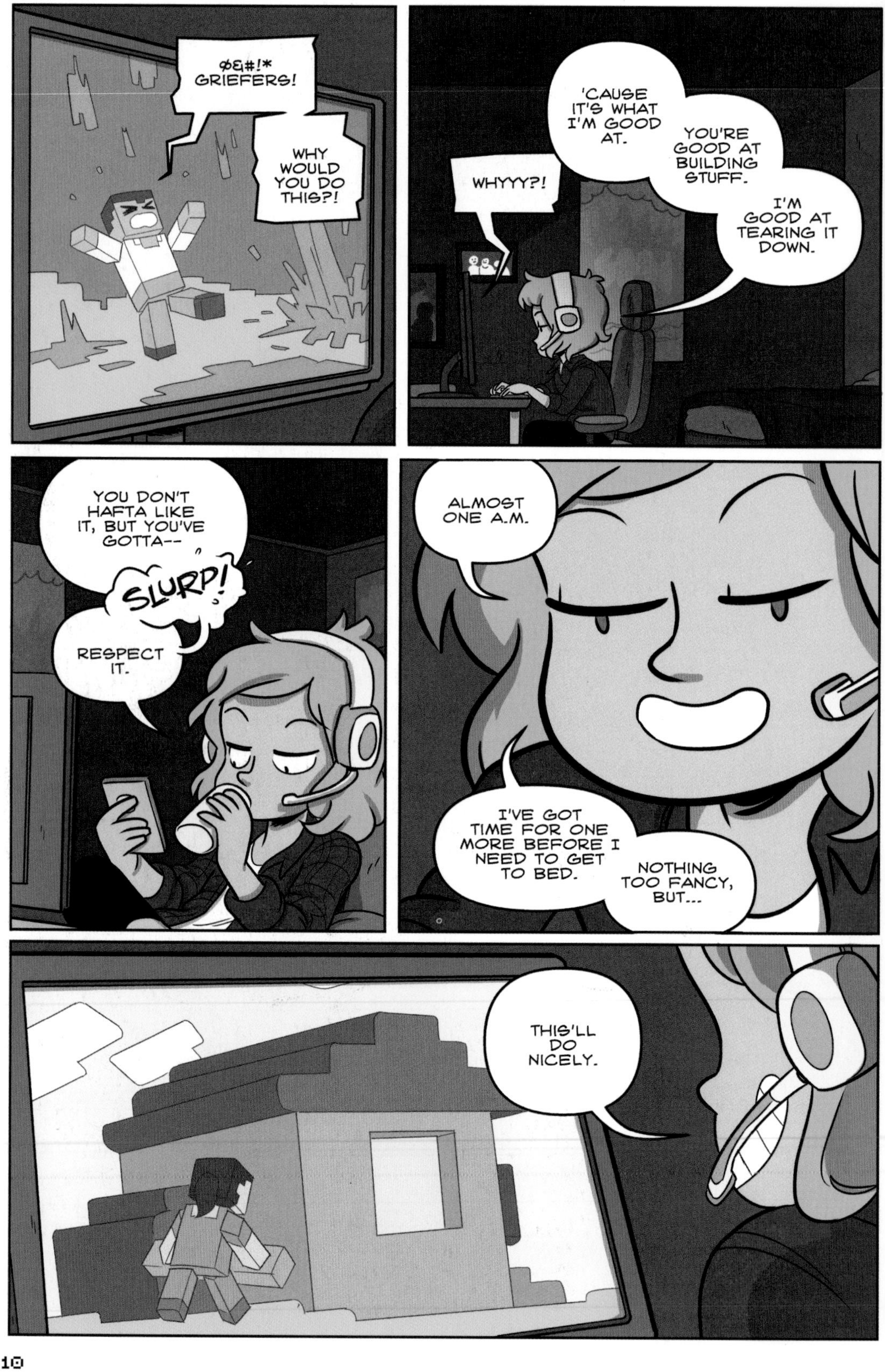

ØƐ#!*
GRIEFERS!
WHY WOULD YOU DO THIS?!
WHYYY?!
'CAUSE IT'S WHAT I'M GOOD AT.
YOU'RE GOOD AT BUILDING STUFF.
I'M GOOD AT TEARING IT DOWN.
YOU DON'T HAFTA LIKE IT, BUT YOU'VE GOTTA--
SLURP!
RESPECT IT.
ALMOST ONE A.M.
I'VE GOT TIME FOR ONE MORE BEFORE I NEED TO GET TO BED.
NOTHING TOO FANCY, BUT...
THIS'LL DO NICELY.

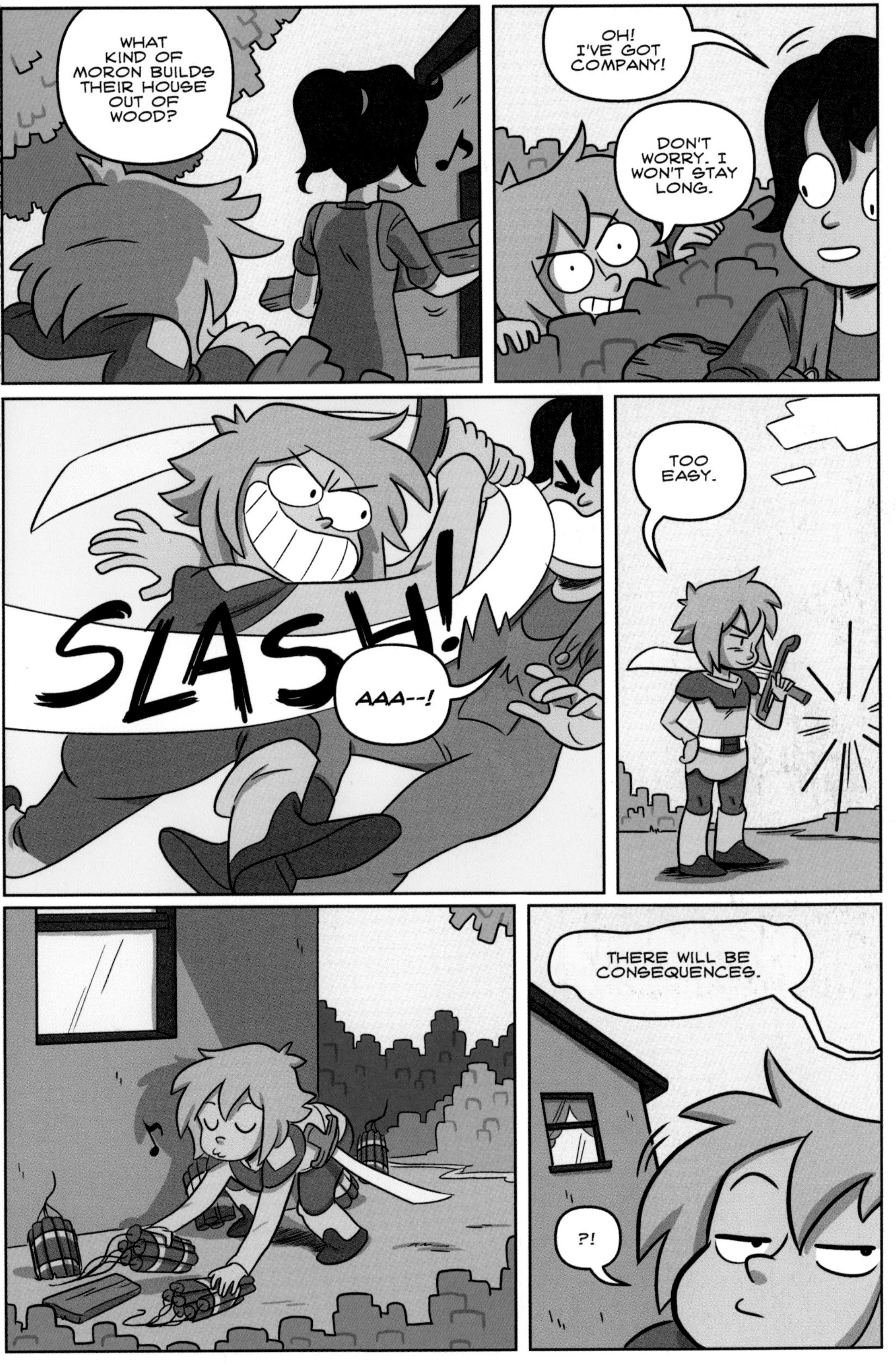
WHAT KIND OF MORON BUILDS THEIR HOUSE OUT OF WOOD?
OH! I'VE GOT COMPANY!
DON'T WORRY. I WON'T STAY LONG.
SLASH!
AAA--!
TOO EASY.
THERE WILL BE CONSEQUENCES.
?!

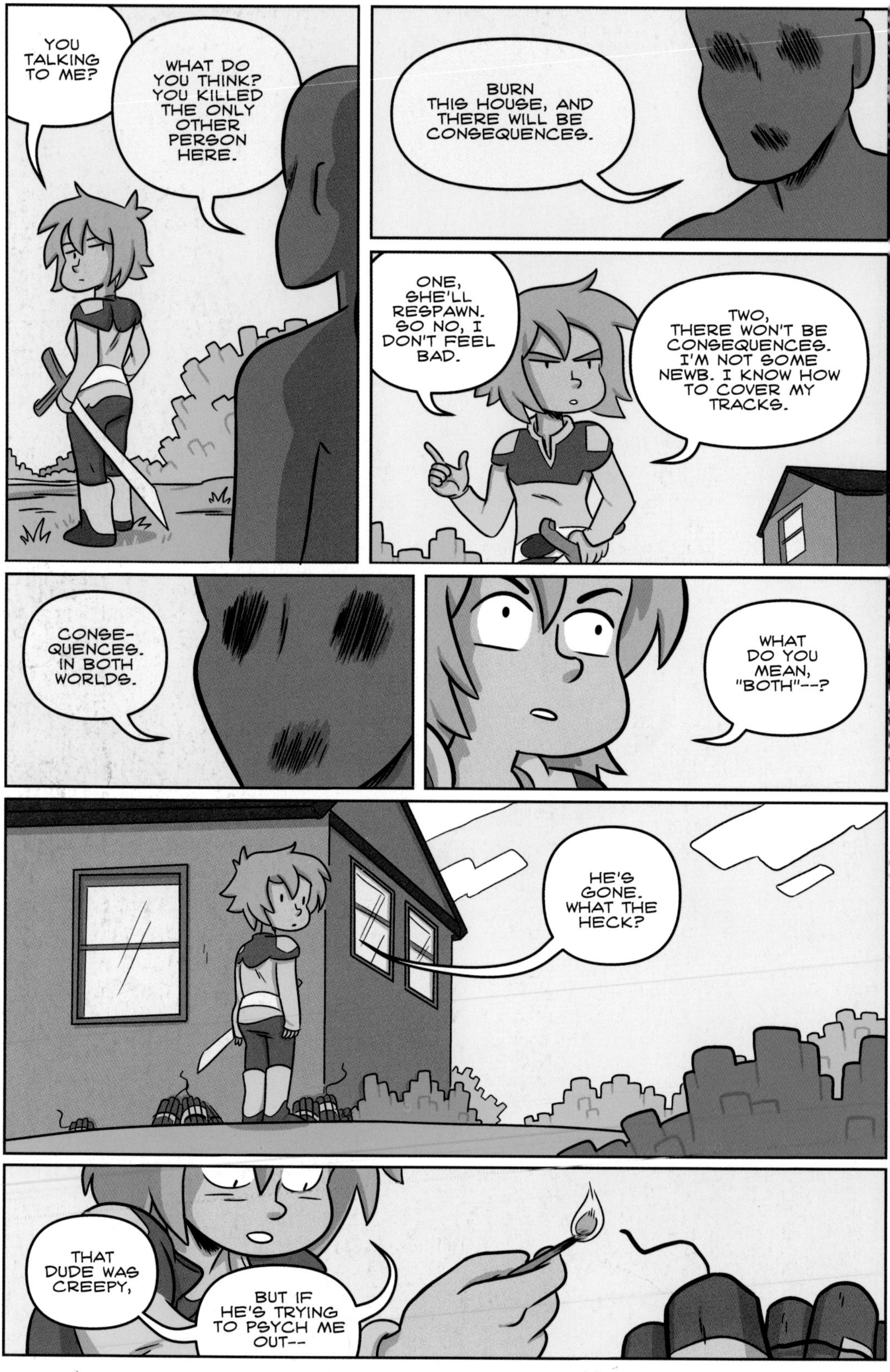
YOU TALKING TO ME?
WHAT DO YOU THINK? YOU KILLED THE ONLY OTHER PERSON HERE.
BURN THIS HOUSE, AND THERE WILL BE CONSEQUENCES.
ONE, SHE'LL RESPAWN. SO NO, I DON'T FEEL BAD.
TWO, THERE WON'T BE CONSEQUENCES. I'M NOT SOME NEWB. I KNOW HOW TO COVER MY TRACKS.
CONSE-QUENCES. IN BOTH WORLDS.
WHAT DO YOU MEAN, "BOTH"--?
HE'S GONE. WHAT THE HECK?
THAT DUDE WAS CREEPY,
BUT IF HE'S TRYING TO PSYCH ME OUT--

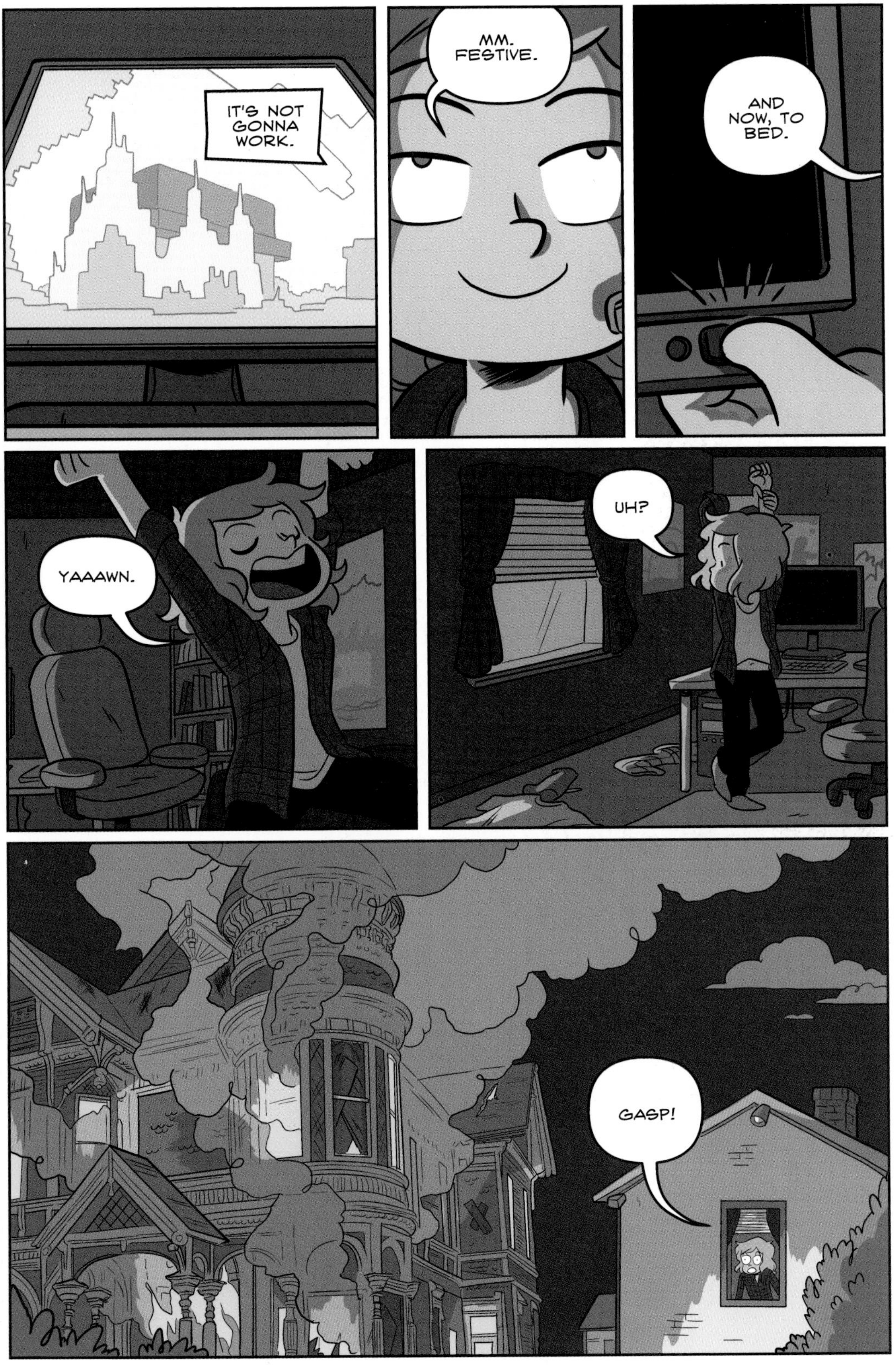
IT'S NOT GONNA WORK.
MM. FESTIVE.
AND NOW, TO BED.
YAAAWN.
UH?
GASP!

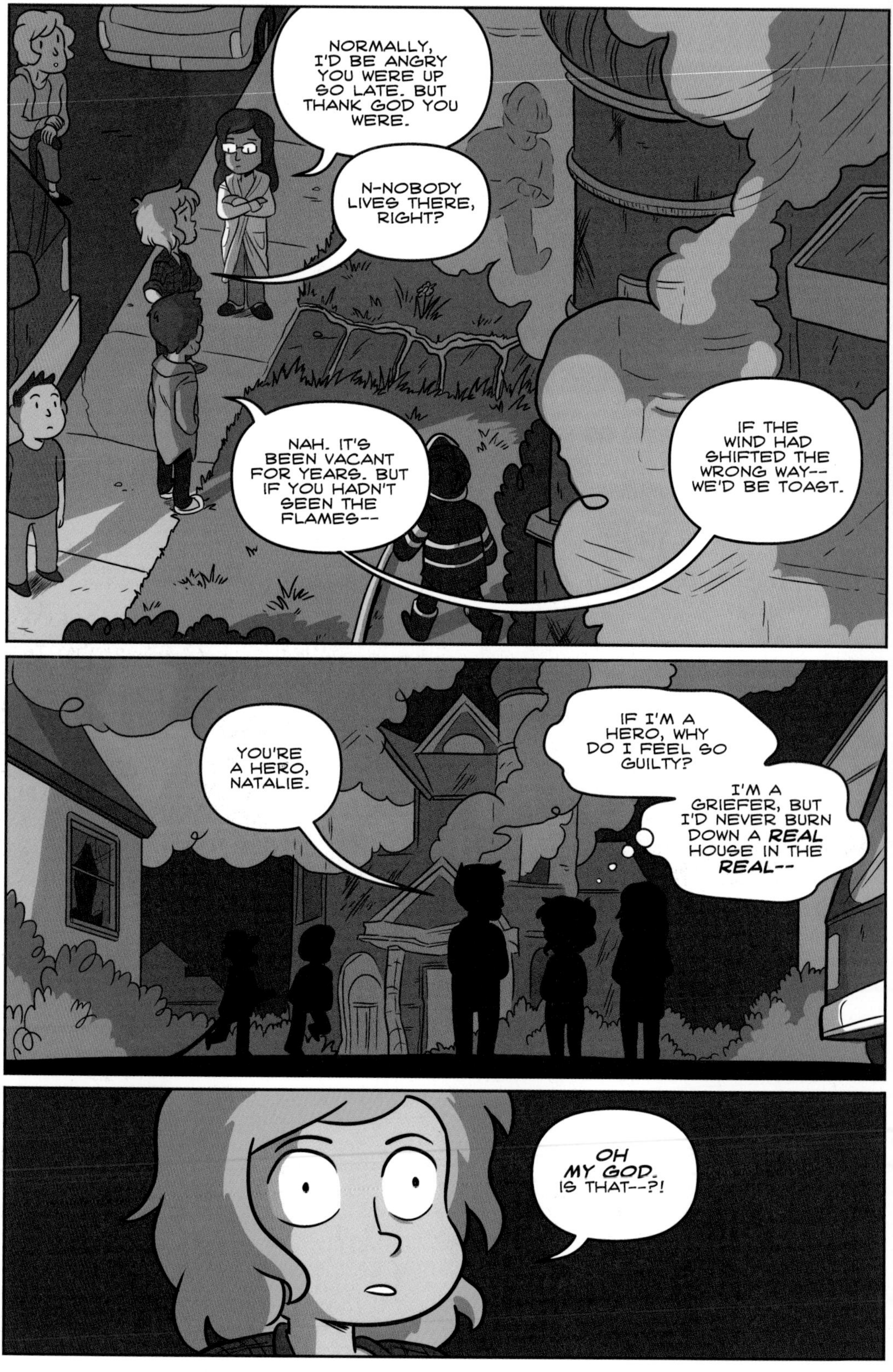
NORMALLY, I'D BE ANGRY YOU WERE UP SO LATE. BUT THANK GOD YOU WERE.
N-NOBODY LIVES THERE, RIGHT?
NAH. IT'S BEEN VACANT FOR YEARS. BUT IF YOU HADN'T SEEN THE FLAMES--
IF THE WIND HAD SHIFTED THE WRONG WAY-- WE'D BE TOAST.
YOU'RE A HERO, NATALIE.
IF I'M A HERO, WHY DO I FEEL SO GUILTY?
I'M A GRIEFER, BUT I'D NEVER BURN DOWN A **REAL** HOUSE IN THE **REAL**--
OH MY GOD. IS THAT--?!

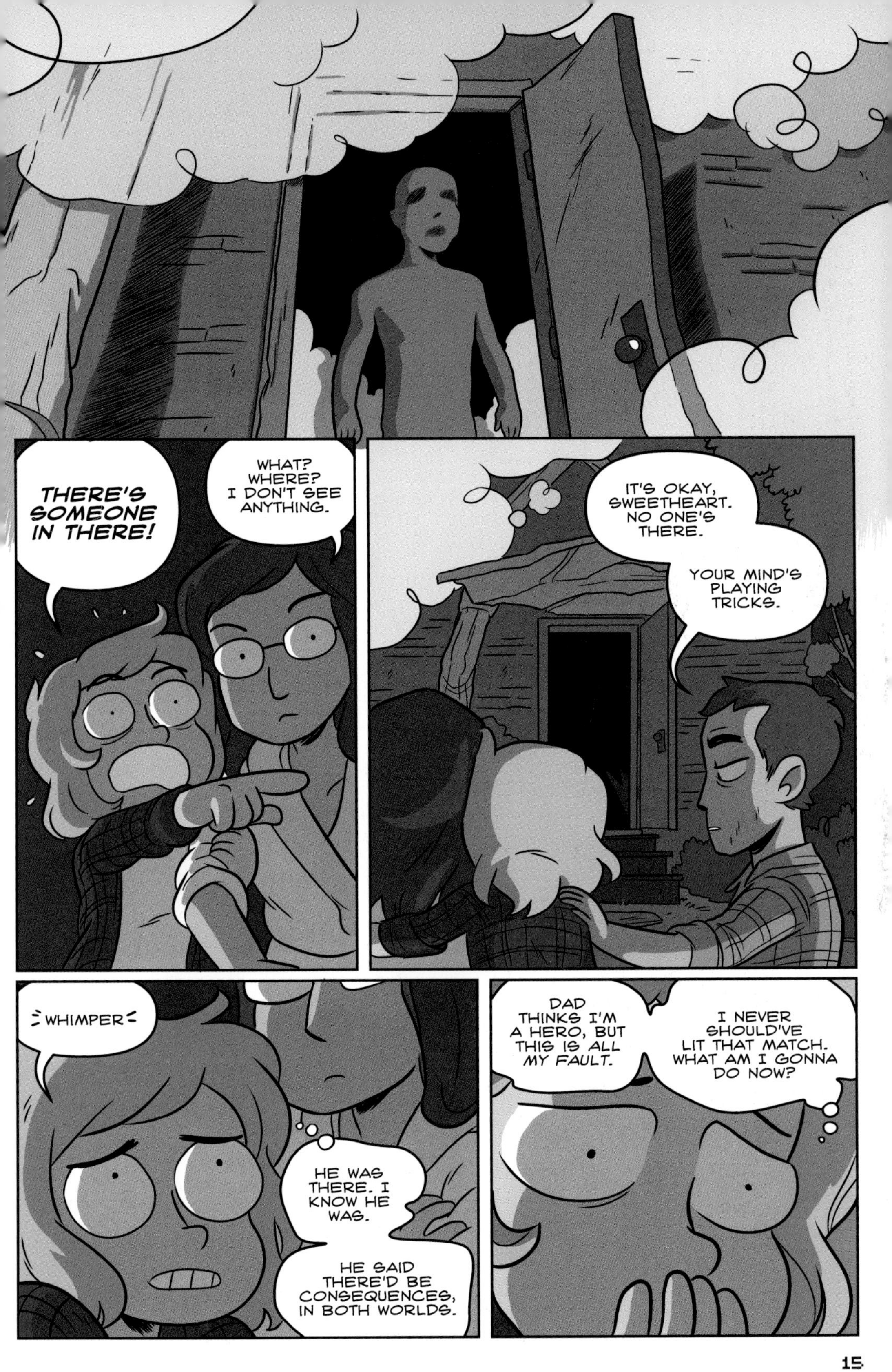
THERE'S SOMEONE IN THERE!
WHAT? WHERE? I DON'T SEE ANYTHING.
IT'S OKAY, SWEETHEART. NO ONE'S THERE.
YOUR MIND'S PLAYING TRICKS.
WHIMPER
HE WAS THERE. I KNOW HE WAS.
HE SAID THERE'D BE CONSEQUENCES, IN BOTH WORLDS.
DAD THINKS I'M A HERO, BUT THIS IS ALL MY FAULT.
I NEVER SHOULD'VE LIT THAT MATCH. WHAT AM I GONNA DO NOW?

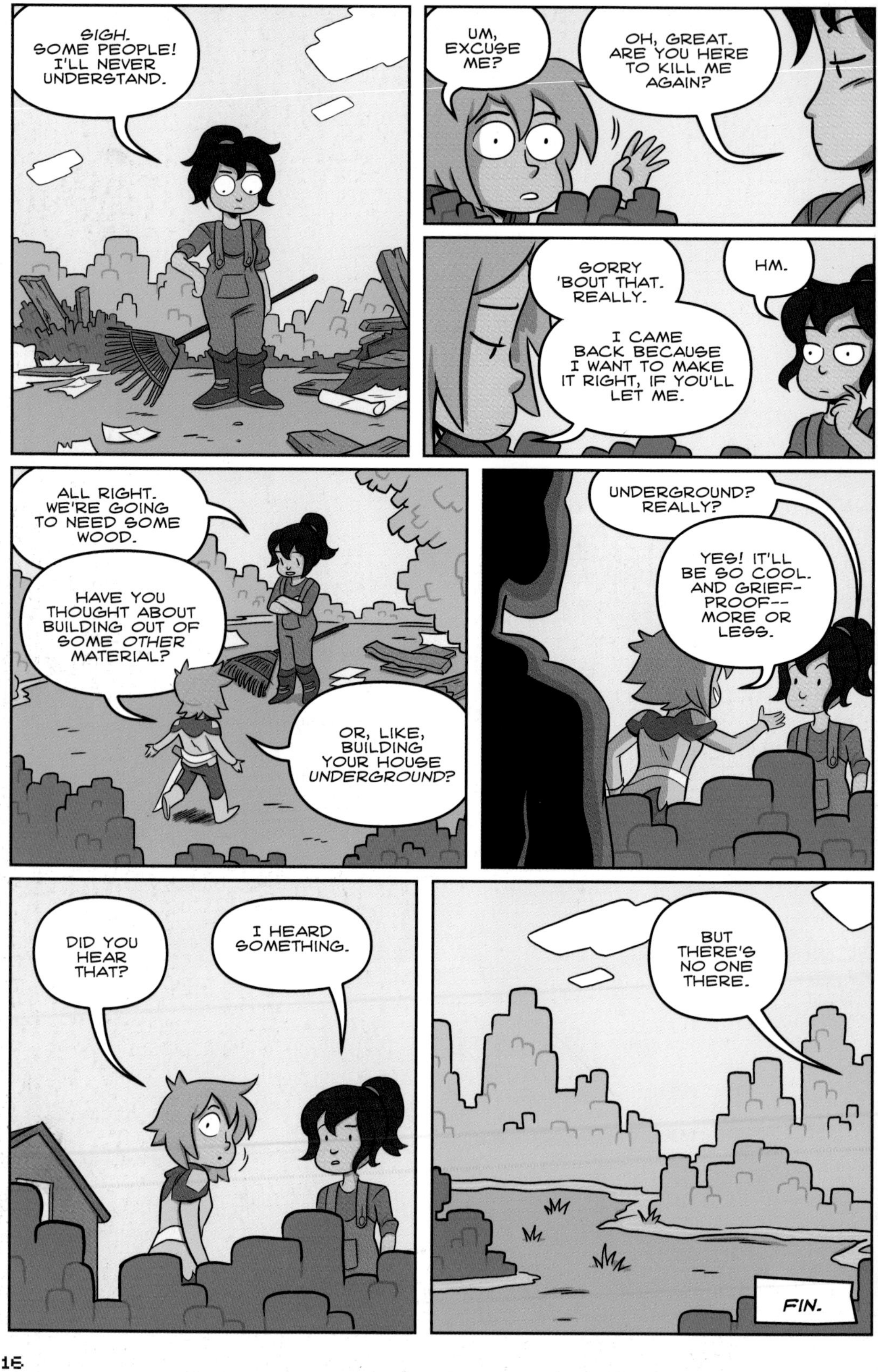
SIGH. SOME PEOPLE! I'LL NEVER UNDERSTAND.
UM, EXCUSE ME?
OH, GREAT. ARE YOU HERE TO KILL ME AGAIN?
SORRY 'BOUT THAT. REALLY.
HM.
I CAME BACK BECAUSE I WANT TO MAKE IT RIGHT, IF YOU'LL LET ME.
ALL RIGHT. WE'RE GOING TO NEED SOME WOOD.
HAVE YOU THOUGHT ABOUT BUILDING OUT OF SOME *OTHER* MATERIAL?
OR, LIKE, BUILDING YOUR HOUSE *UNDERGROUND*?
UNDERGROUND? REALLY?
YES! IT'LL BE SO COOL. AND GRIEF-PROOF-- MORE OR LESS.
DID YOU HEAR THAT?
I HEARD SOMETHING.
BUT THERE'S NO ONE THERE.
FIN.

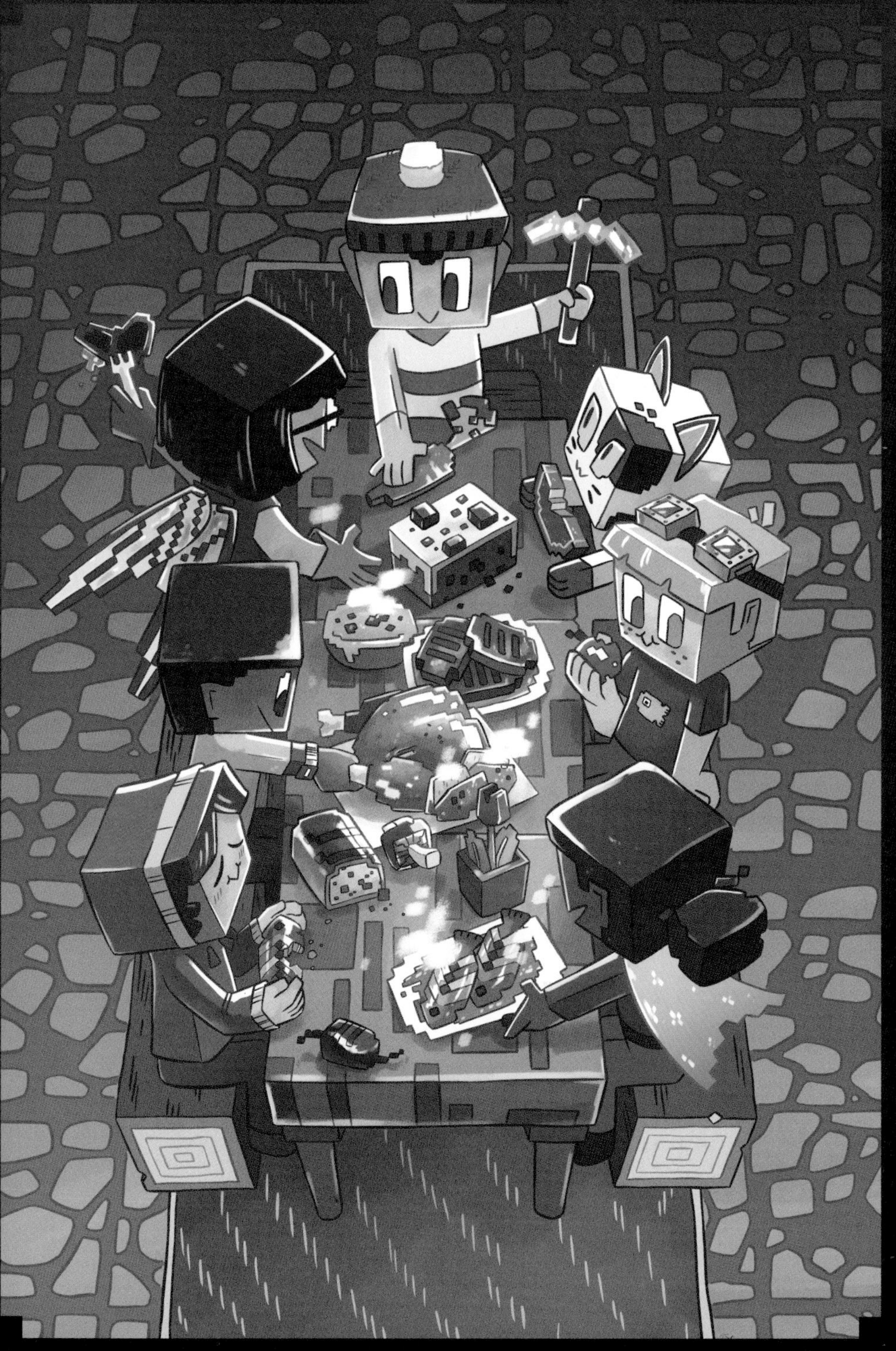

ILLUSTRATION BY

NATALIE RIESS

BIRTHDAY BOY

STORY BY
KEVIN PANETTA

ART AND LETTERING BY
SAVANNA GANUCHEAU

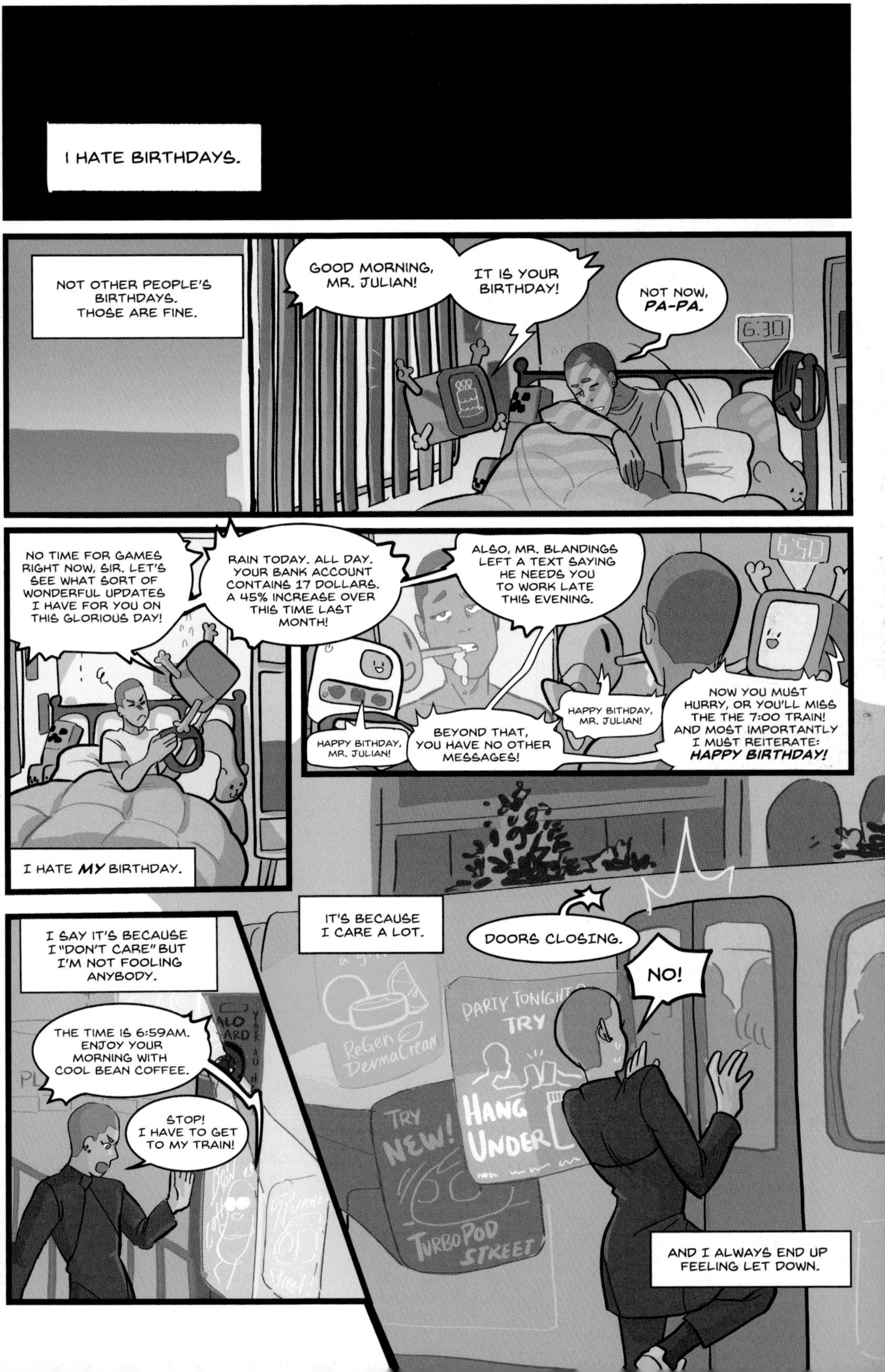
I HATE BIRTHDAYS.
NOT OTHER PEOPLE'S BIRTHDAYS. THOSE ARE FINE.
GOOD MORNING, MR. JULIAN!
IT IS YOUR BIRTHDAY!
NOT NOW, *PA-PA.*
6:30
NO TIME FOR GAMES RIGHT NOW, SIR. LET'S SEE WHAT SORT OF WONDERFUL UPDATES I HAVE FOR YOU ON THIS GLORIOUS DAY!
RAIN TODAY. ALL DAY. YOUR BANK ACCOUNT CONTAINS 17 DOLLARS. A 45% INCREASE OVER THIS TIME LAST MONTH!
ALSO, MR. BLANDINGS LEFT A TEXT SAYING HE NEEDS YOU TO WORK LATE THIS EVENING.
6:50
HAPPY BITHDAY, MR. JULIAN!
BEYOND THAT, YOU HAVE NO OTHER MESSAGES!
HAPPY BITHDAY, MR. JULIAN!
NOW YOU MUST HURRY, OR YOU'LL MISS THE THE 7:00 TRAIN! AND MOST IMPORTANTLY I MUST REITERATE: ***HAPPY BIRTHDAY!***
I HATE ***MY*** BIRTHDAY.
I SAY IT'S BECAUSE I "DON'T CARE" BUT I'M NOT FOOLING ANYBODY.
IT'S BECAUSE I CARE A LOT.
DOORS CLOSING.
NO!
THE TIME IS 6:59AM. ENJOY YOUR MORNING WITH COOL BEAN COFFEE.
STOP! I HAVE TO GET TO MY TRAIN!
ReGen DermaCream
PARTY TONIGHT? TRY HANG UNDER
TRY NEW! TURBOPOD STREET
AND I ALWAYS END UP FEELING LET DOWN.

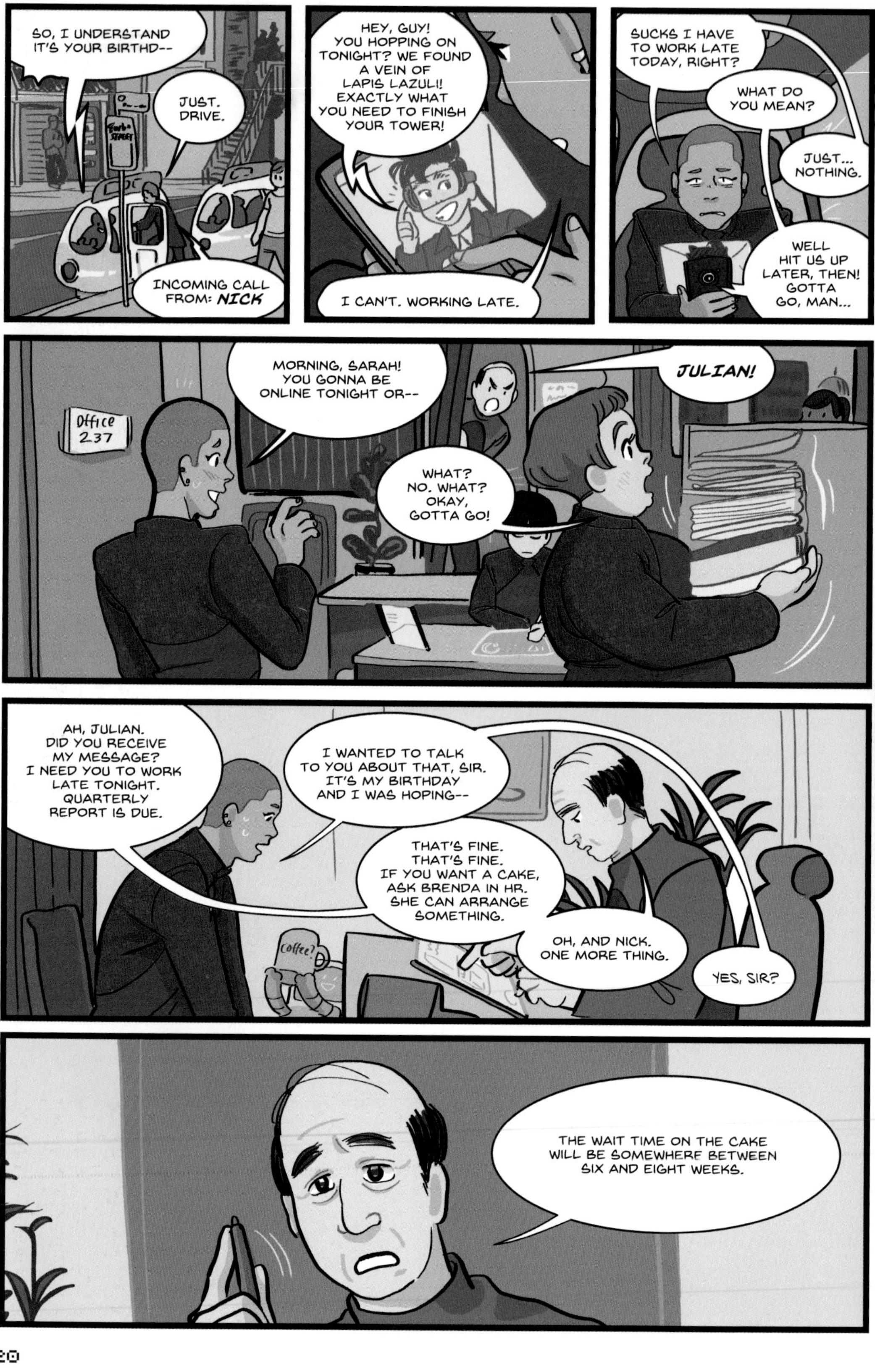
SO, I UNDERSTAND IT'S YOUR BIRTHD--
JUST. DRIVE.
INCOMING CALL FROM: NICK
HEY, GUY! YOU HOPPING ON TONIGHT? WE FOUND A VEIN OF LAPIS LAZULI! EXACTLY WHAT YOU NEED TO FINISH YOUR TOWER!
I CAN'T. WORKING LATE.
SUCKS I HAVE TO WORK LATE TODAY, RIGHT?
WHAT DO YOU MEAN?
JUST... NOTHING.
WELL HIT US UP LATER, THEN! GOTTA GO, MAN...
Office 237
MORNING, SARAH! YOU GONNA BE ONLINE TONIGHT OR--
JULIAN!
WHAT? NO. WHAT? OKAY, GOTTA GO!
AH, JULIAN. DID YOU RECEIVE MY MESSAGE? I NEED YOU TO WORK LATE TONIGHT. QUARTERLY REPORT IS DUE.
I WANTED TO TALK TO YOU ABOUT THAT, SIR. IT'S MY BIRTHDAY AND I WAS HOPING--
THAT'S FINE. THAT'S FINE. IF YOU WANT A CAKE, ASK BRENDA IN HR. SHE CAN ARRANGE SOMETHING.
Coffee?
OH, AND NICK. ONE MORE THING.
YES, SIR?
THE WAIT TIME ON THE CAKE WILL BE SOMEWHERE BETWEEN SIX AND EIGHT WEEKS.

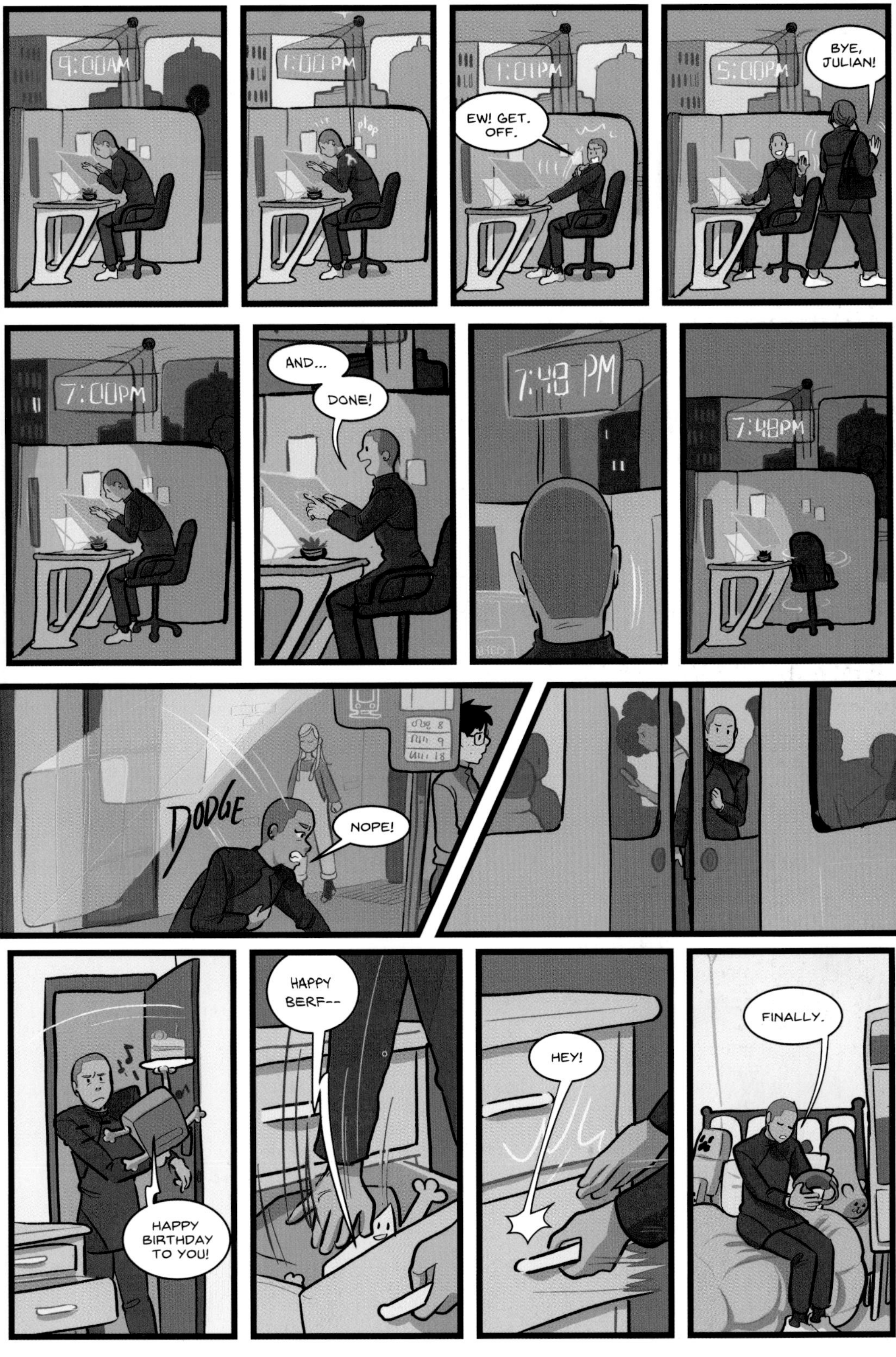
9:00AM
1:00 PM
plop
1:01PM
EW! GET. OFF.
5:00PM
BYE, JULIAN!
7:00PM
AND...
DONE!
7:48 PM
7:48PM
DODGE
NOPE!
HAPPY BIRTHDAY TO YOU!
HAPPY BERF--
HEY!
FINALLY.

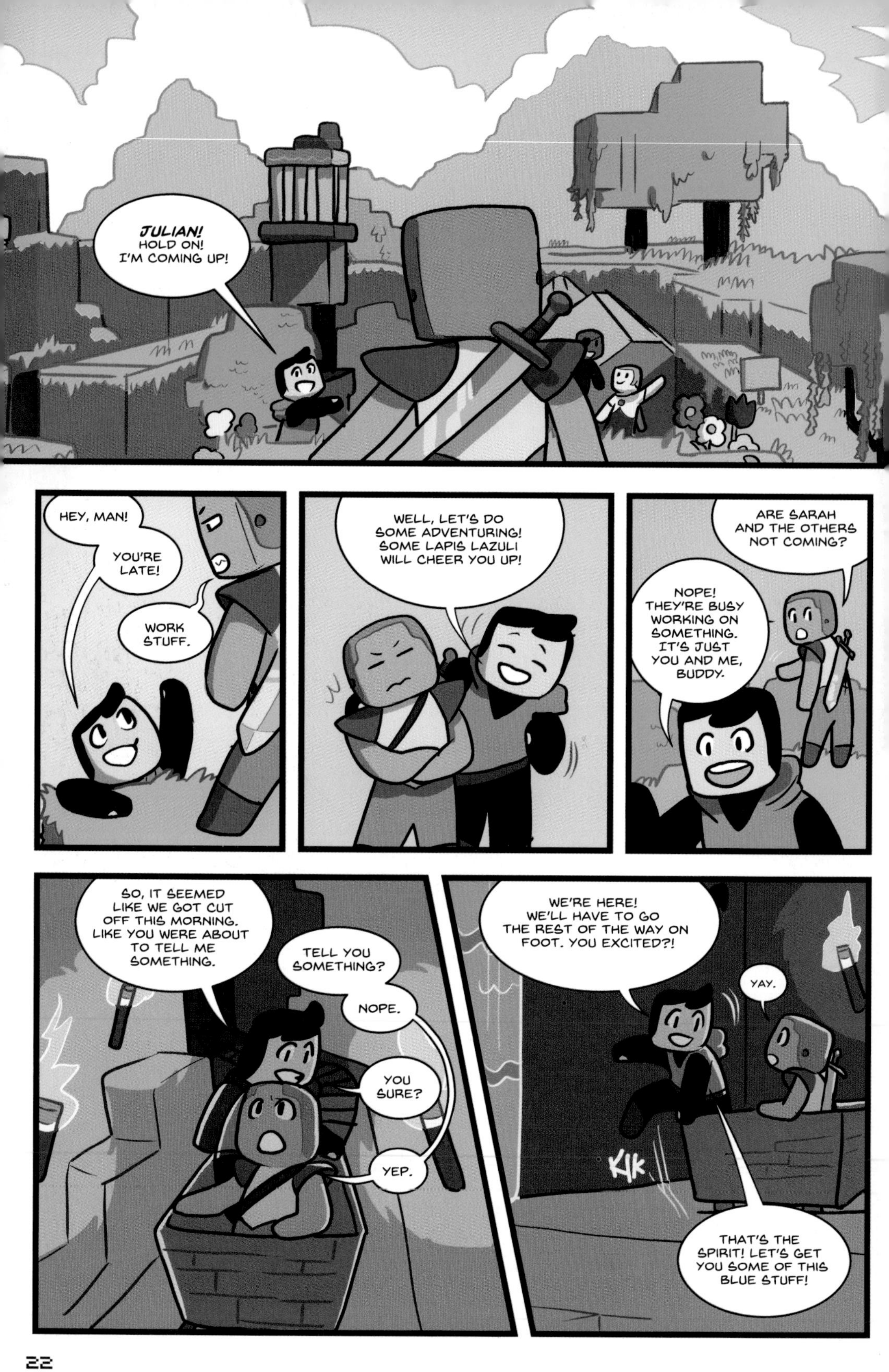

JULIAN! HOLD ON! I'M COMING UP!
HEY, MAN!
YOU'RE LATE!
WORK STUFF.
WELL, LET'S DO SOME ADVENTURING! SOME LAPIS LAZULI WILL CHEER YOU UP!
ARE SARAH AND THE OTHERS NOT COMING?
NOPE! THEY'RE BUSY WORKING ON SOMETHING. IT'S JUST YOU AND ME, BUDDY.
SO, IT SEEMED LIKE WE GOT CUT OFF THIS MORNING. LIKE YOU WERE ABOUT TO TELL ME SOMETHING.
TELL YOU SOMETHING?
NOPE.
YOU SURE?
YEP.
WE'RE HERE! WE'LL HAVE TO GO THE REST OF THE WAY ON FOOT. YOU EXCITED?!
YAY.
KIK
THAT'S THE SPIRIT! LET'S GET YOU SOME OF THIS BLUE STUFF!

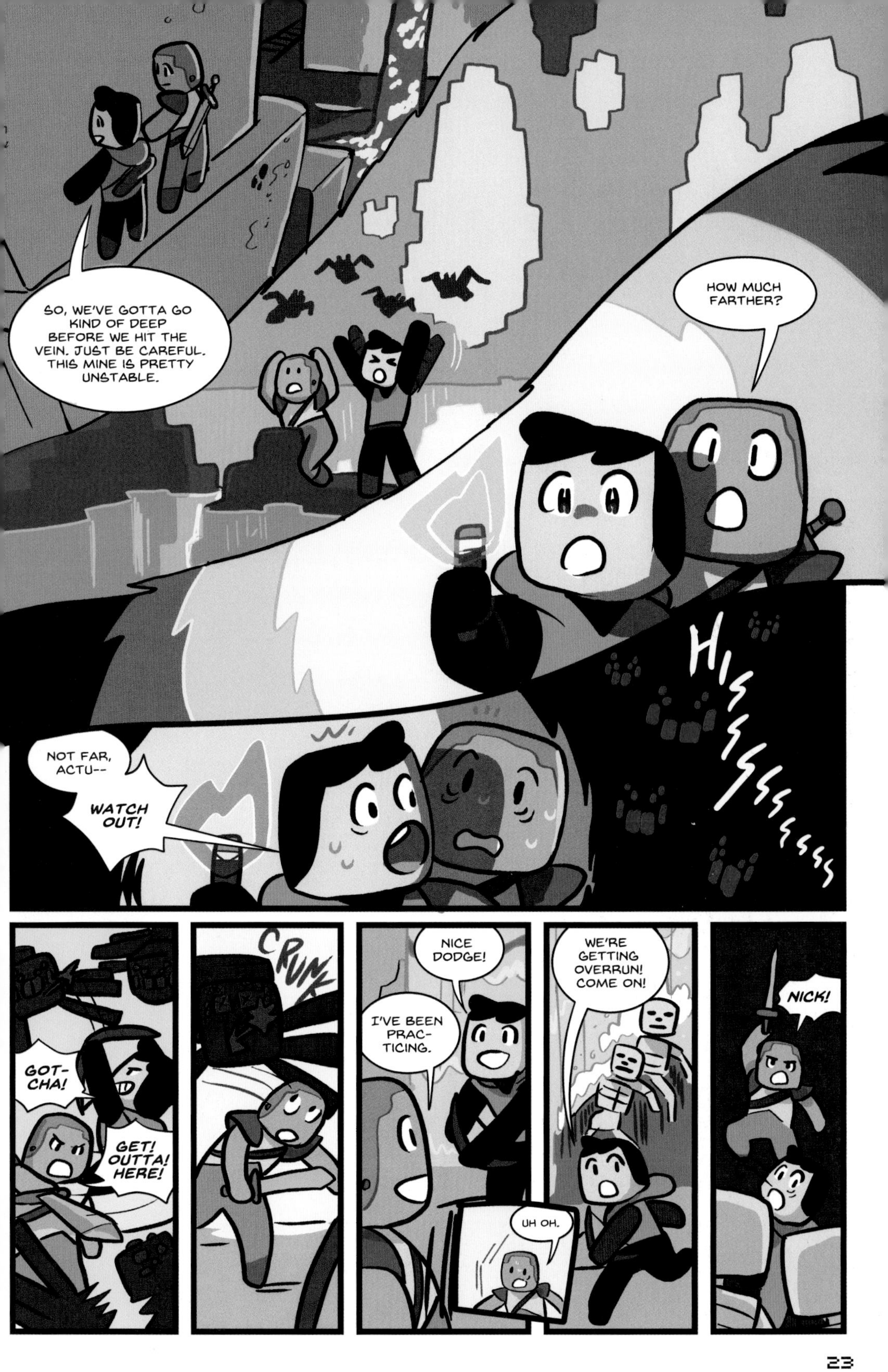
SO, WE'VE GOTTA GO KIND OF DEEP BEFORE WE HIT THE VEIN. JUST BE CAREFUL. THIS MINE IS PRETTY UNSTABLE.
HOW MUCH FARTHER?
NOT FAR, ACTU--
WATCH OUT!
HISSSSSSSS
GOT-CHA!
GET! OUTTA! HERE!
CRUNK
NICE DODGE!
I'VE BEEN PRAC-TICING.
WE'RE GETTING OVERRUN! COME ON!
UH OH.
NICK!

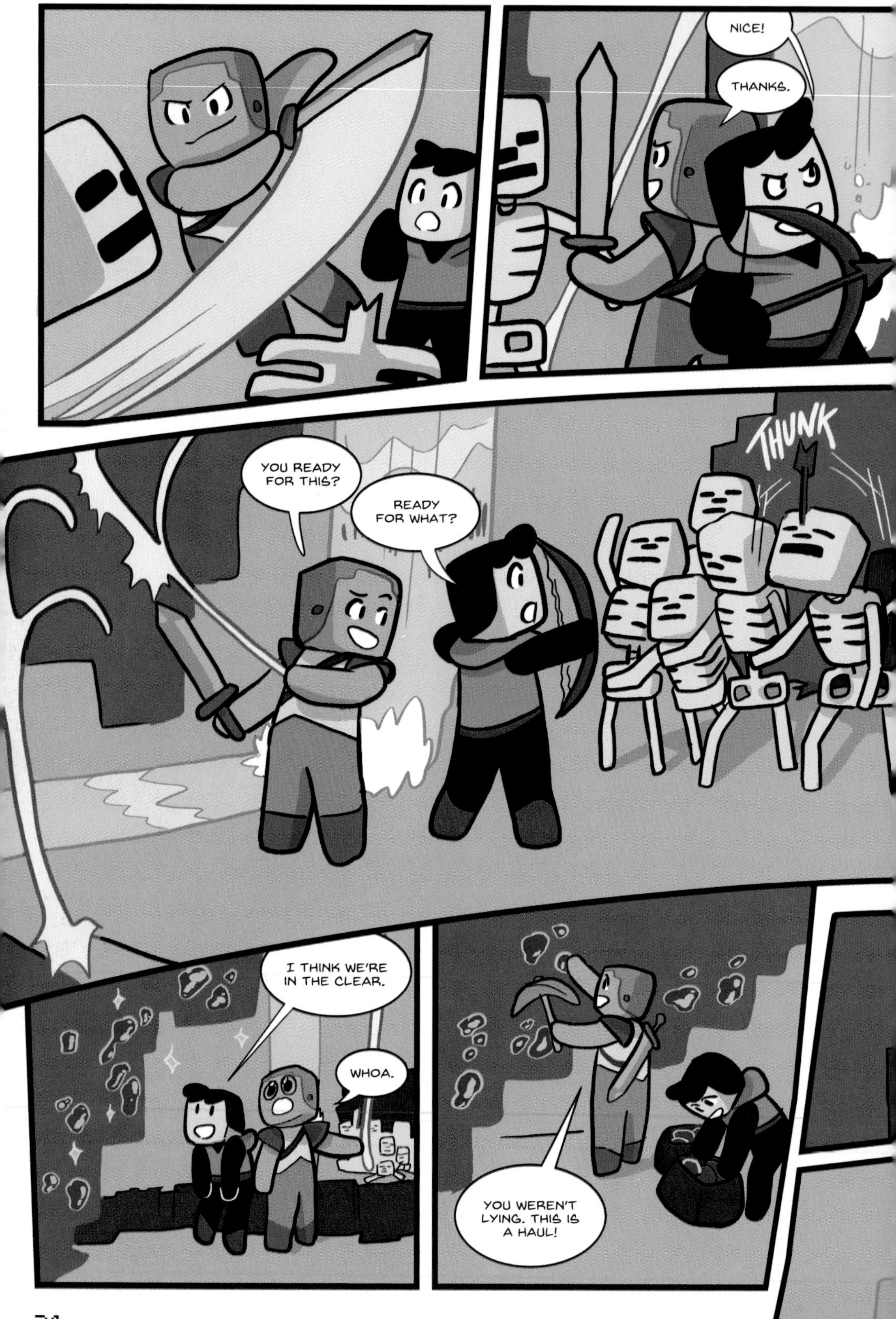
NICE!
THANKS.
YOU READY FOR THIS?
READY FOR WHAT?
THUNK
I THINK WE'RE IN THE CLEAR.
WHOA.
YOU WEREN'T LYING. THIS IS A HAUL!

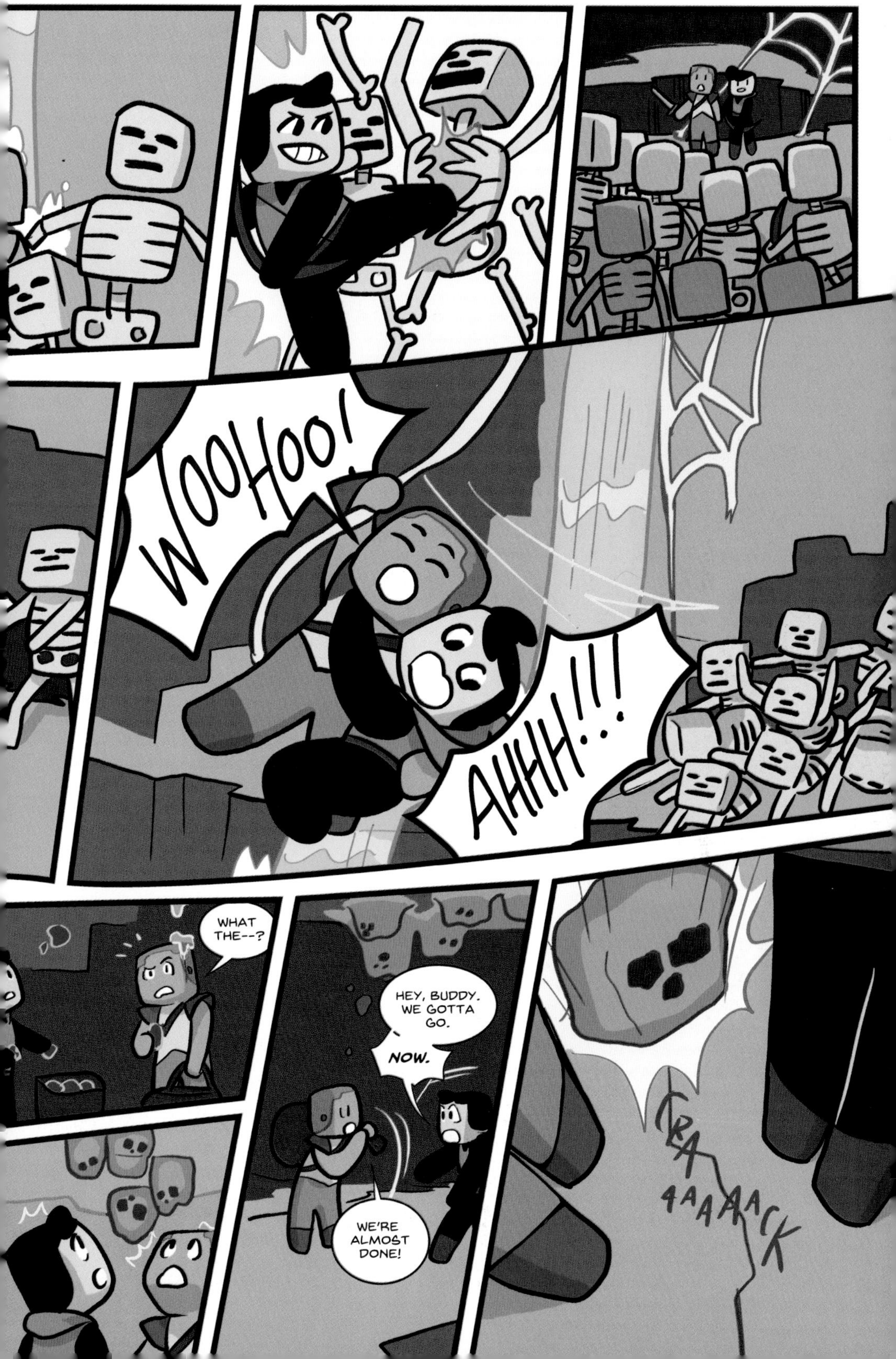
WOOHOO!
AHHH!!!
WHAT THE--?
HEY, BUDDY. WE GOTTA GO.
NOW.
WE'RE ALMOST DONE!
CRAAAAAACK

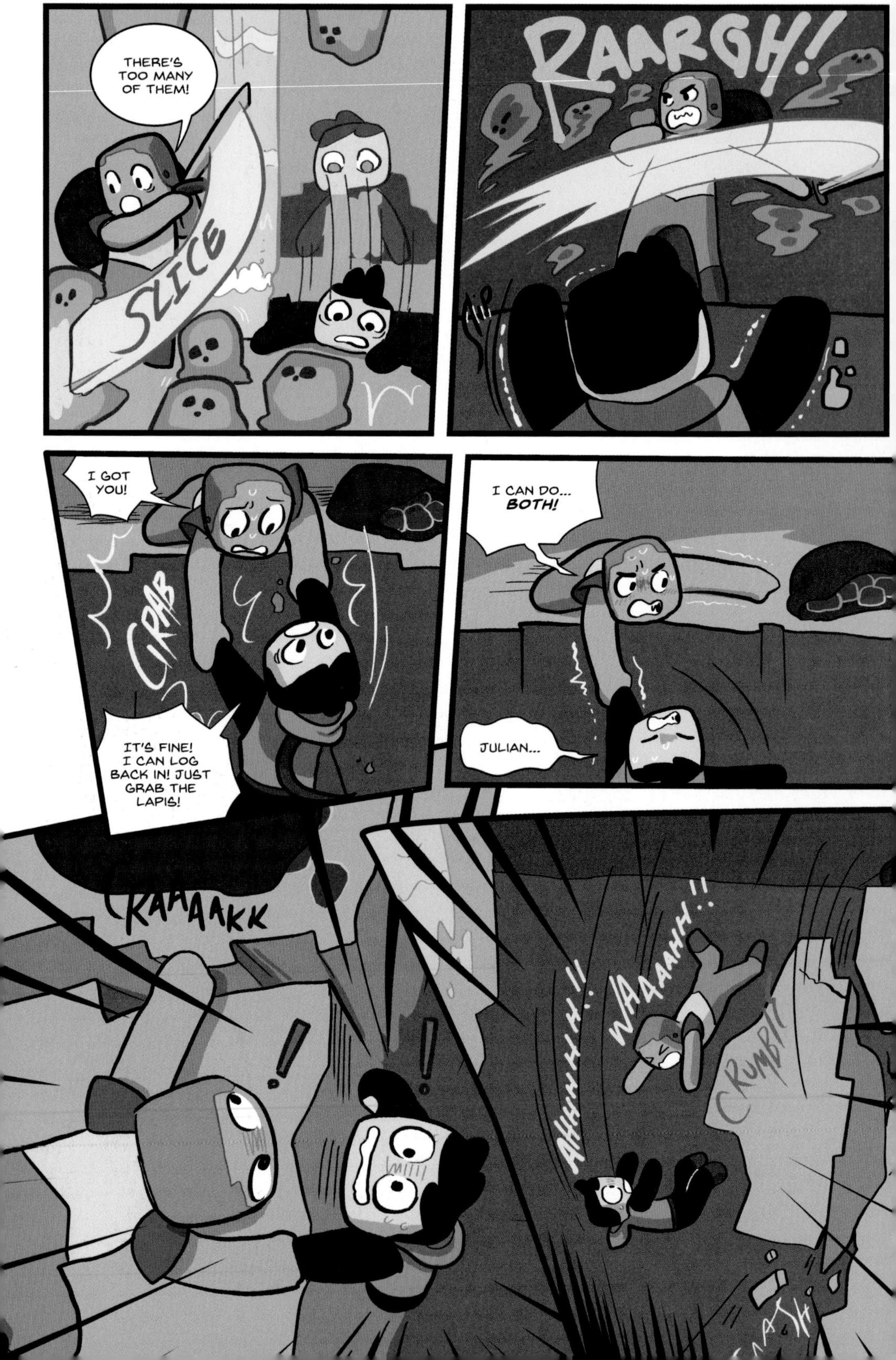
THERE'S TOO MANY OF THEM!
SLICE
RAARGH!
I GOT YOU!
GRAB
IT'S FINE! I CAN LOG BACK IN! JUST GRAB THE LAPIS!
I CAN DO... BOTH!
JULIAN...
KRAAAAKK
AHHHHHH!!
WAAAAHH!!
CRUMBL
CRASH

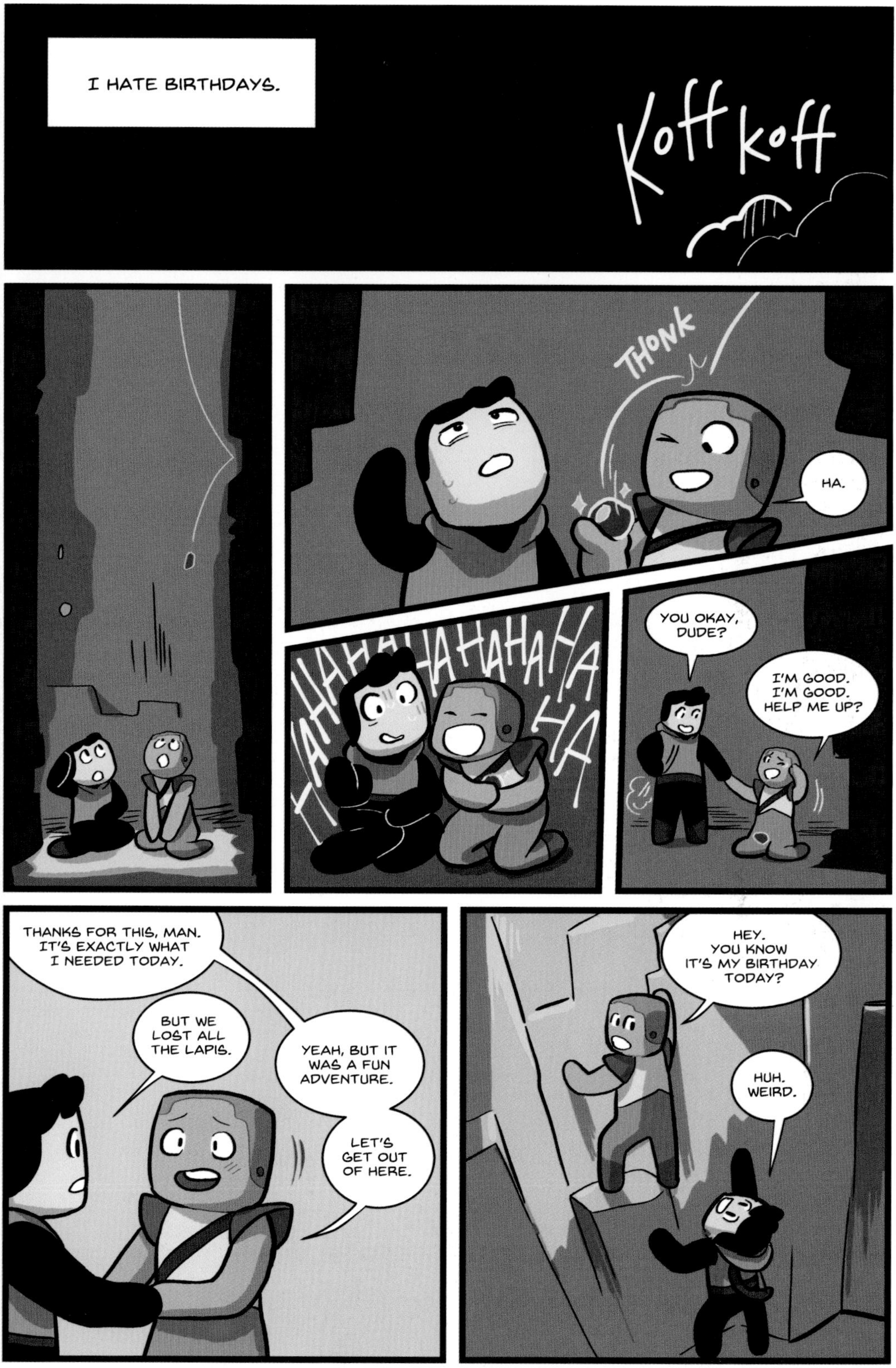
I HATE BIRTHDAYS.
Koff koff
THONK
HA.
HAHAHAHAHAHAHAHA
YOU OKAY, DUDE?
I'M GOOD. I'M GOOD. HELP ME UP?
THANKS FOR THIS, MAN. IT'S EXACTLY WHAT I NEEDED TODAY.
BUT WE LOST ALL THE LAPIS.
YEAH, BUT IT WAS A FUN ADVENTURE.
LET'S GET OUT OF HERE.
HEY. YOU KNOW IT'S MY BIRTHDAY TODAY?
HUH. WEIRD.

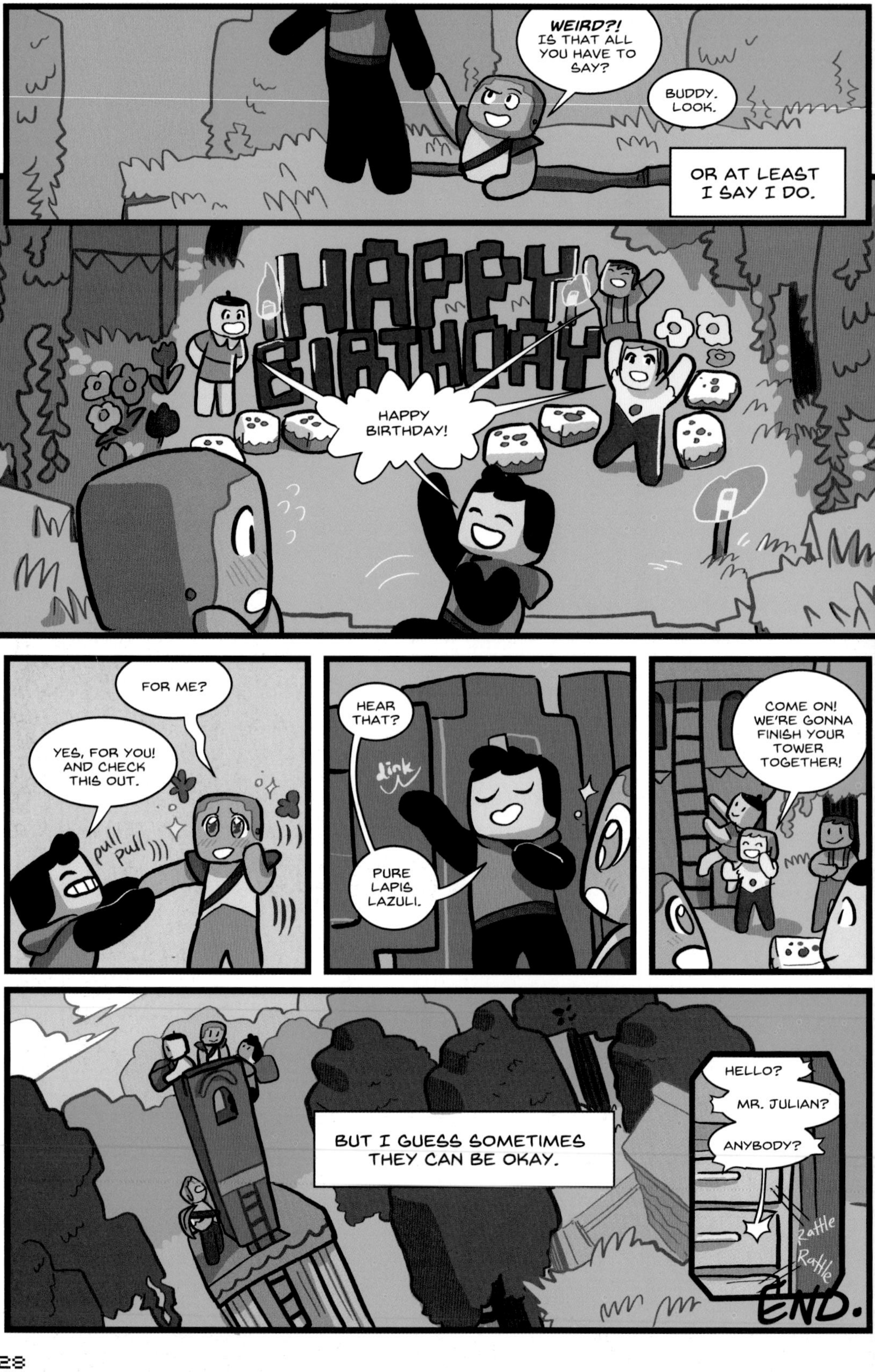
WEIRD?! IS THAT ALL YOU HAVE TO SAY?
BUDDY. LOOK.
OR AT LEAST I SAY I DO.
HAPPY BIRTHDAY
HAPPY BIRTHDAY!
FOR ME?
YES, FOR YOU! AND CHECK THIS OUT.
pull pull
HEAR THAT?
dink
PURE LAPIS LAZULI.
COME ON! WE'RE GONNA FINISH YOUR TOWER TOGETHER!
BUT I GUESS SOMETIMES THEY CAN BE OKAY.
HELLO?
MR. JULIAN?
ANYBODY?
Rattle
Rattle
END.

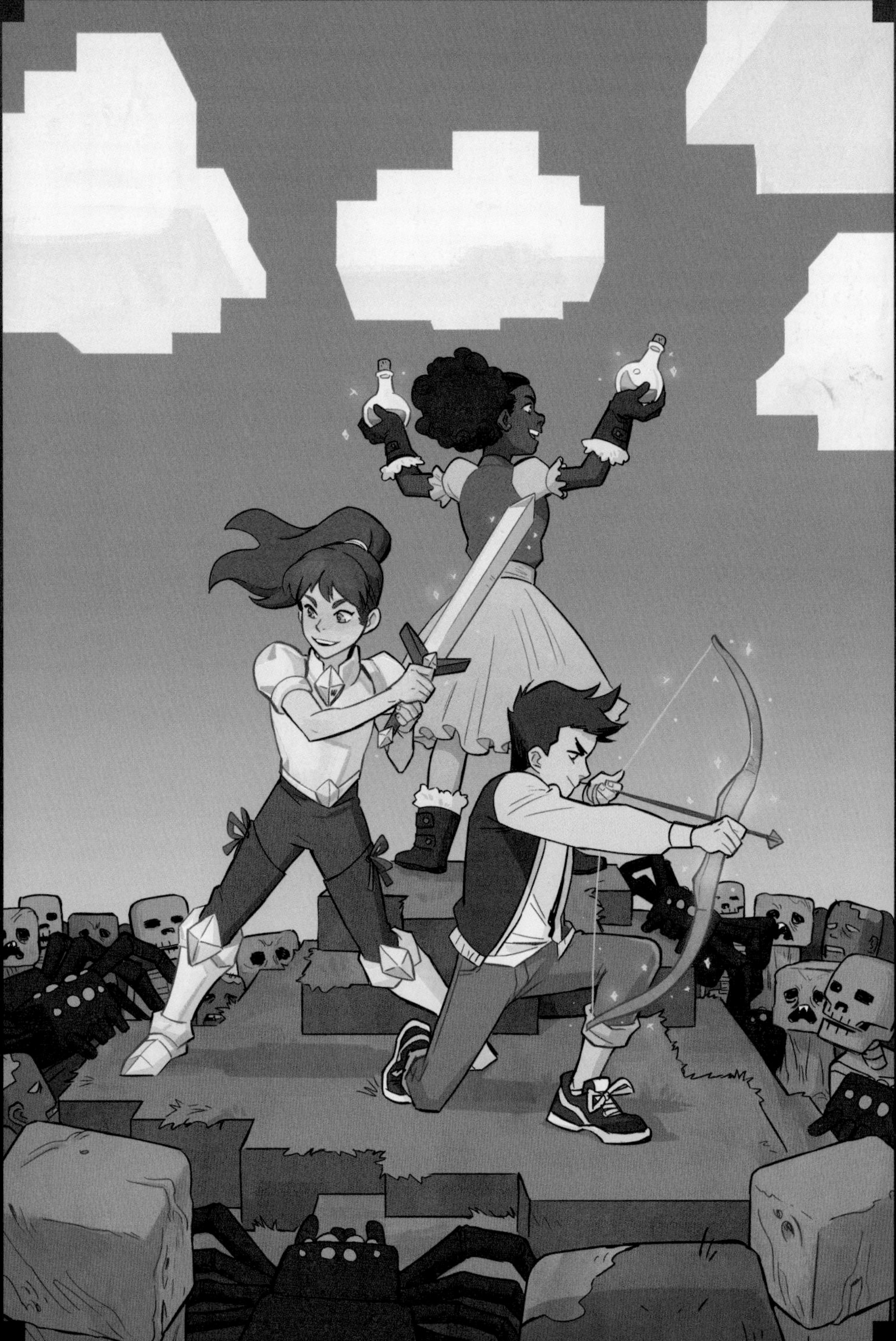

ILLUSTRATION BY

MICHELLE WONG

A CREEPER'S TALE

STORY BY
RYAN NORTH

ART AND LETTERING BY
CHERYL YOUNG

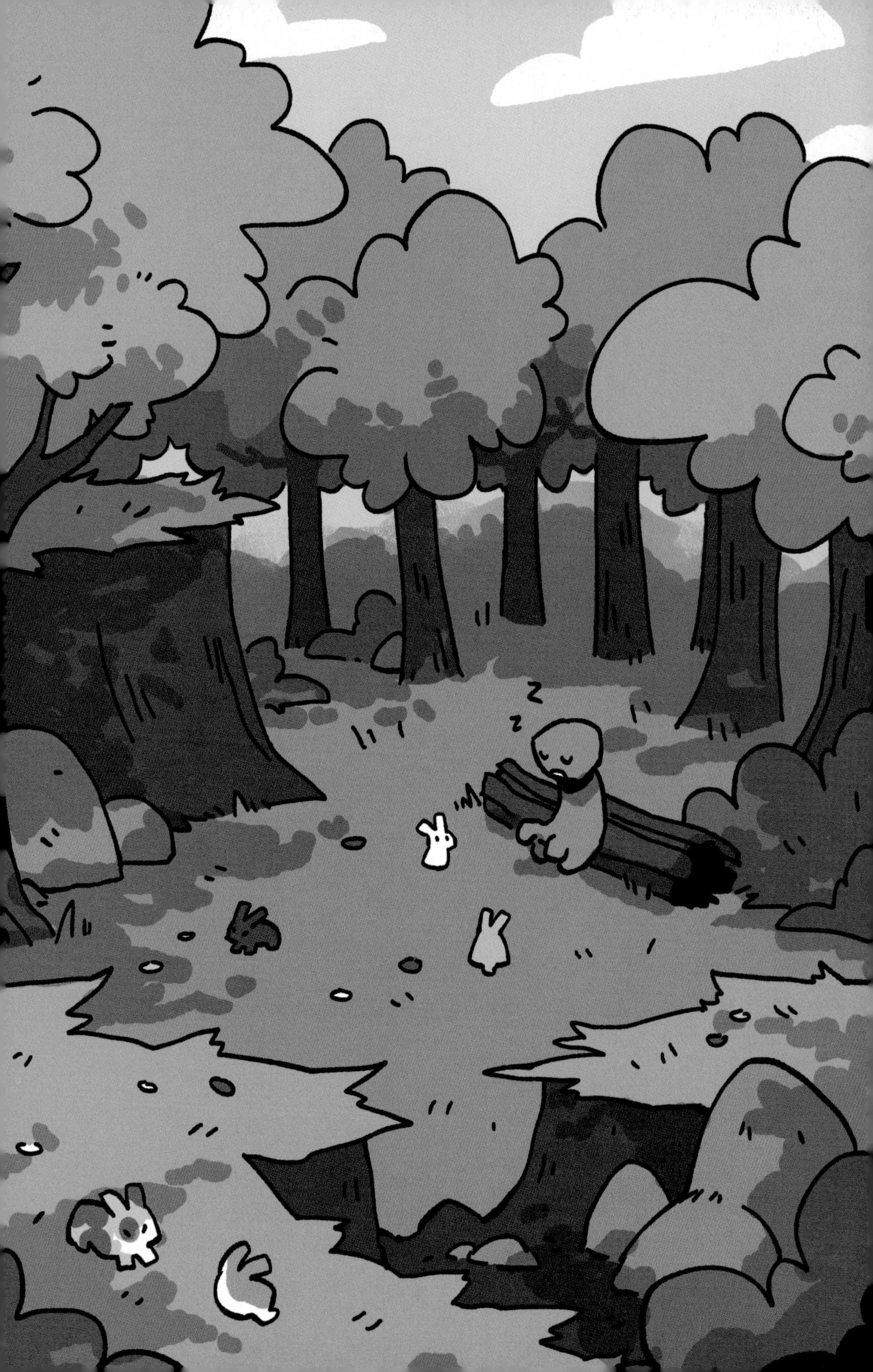
Z
Z

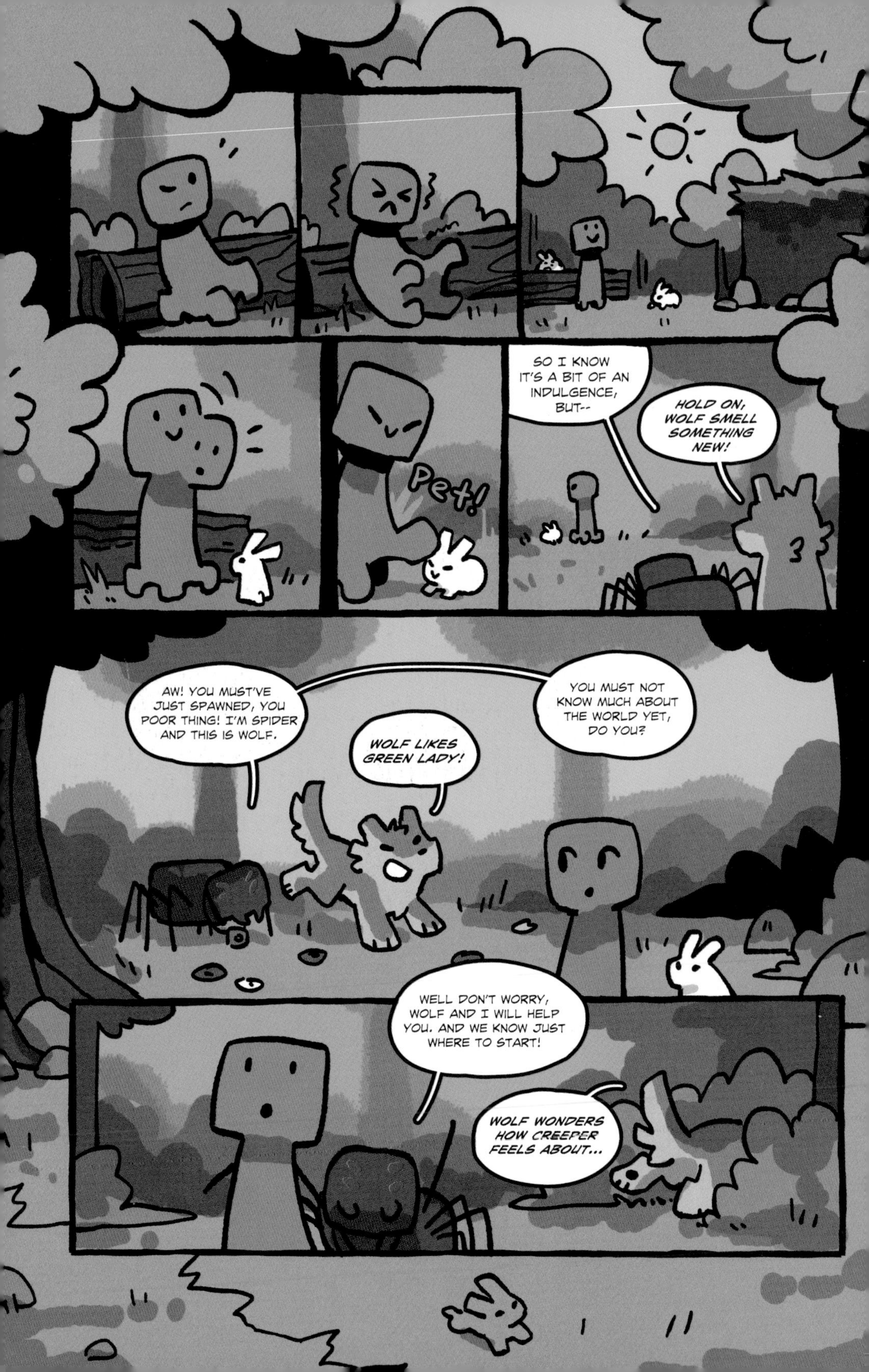
Pet!
SO I KNOW IT'S A BIT OF AN INDULGENCE, BUT--
HOLD ON, WOLF SMELL SOMETHING NEW!
AW! YOU MUST'VE JUST SPAWNED, YOU POOR THING! I'M SPIDER AND THIS IS WOLF.
WOLF LIKES GREEN LADY!
YOU MUST NOT KNOW MUCH ABOUT THE WORLD YET, DO YOU?
WELL DON'T WORRY, WOLF AND I WILL HELP YOU. AND WE KNOW JUST WHERE TO START!
WOLF WONDERS HOW CREEPER FEELS ABOUT...

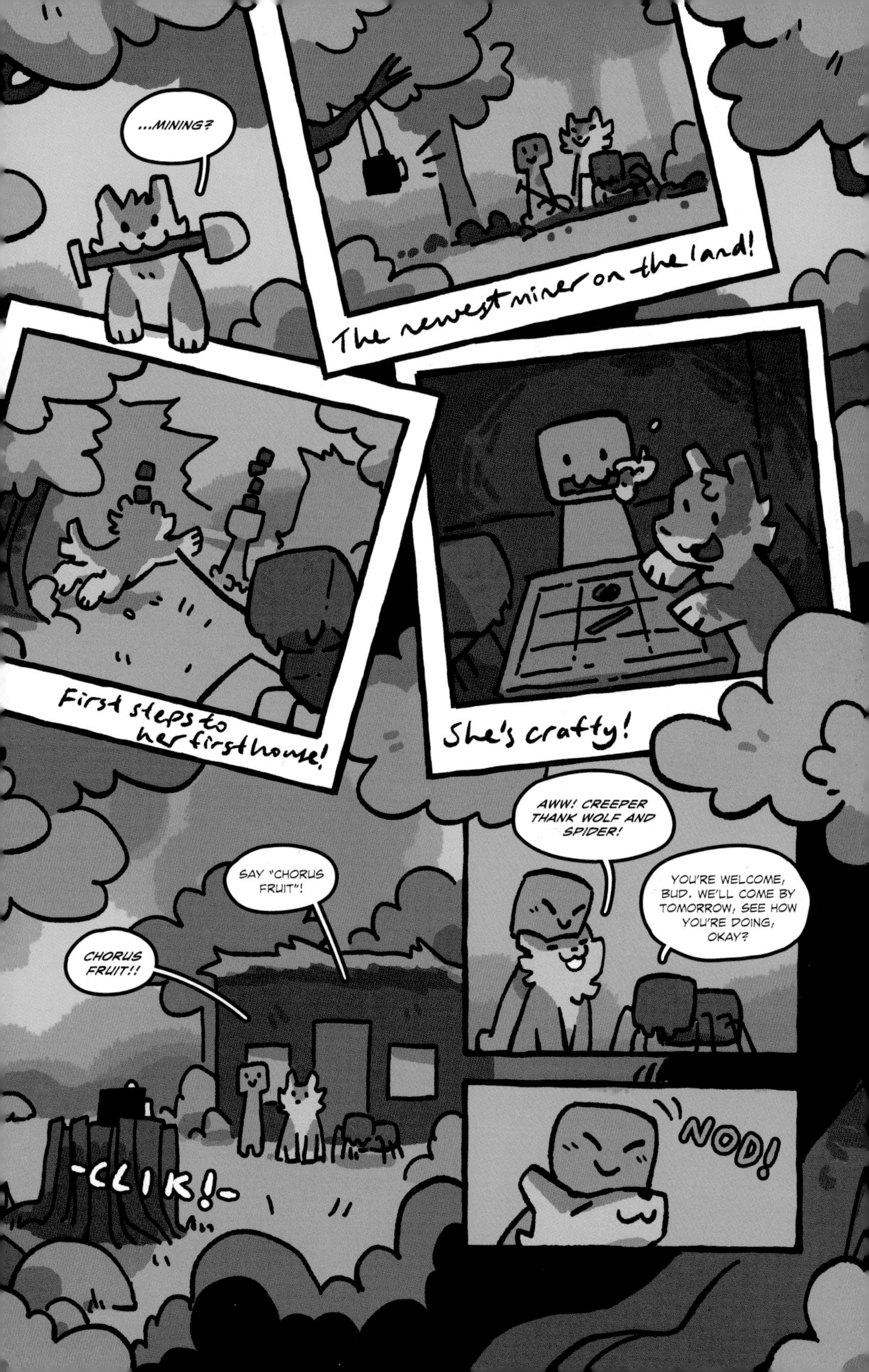
...MINING?
The newest miner on the land!
First steps to her first house!
She's crafty!
SAY "CHORUS FRUIT"!
CHORUS FRUIT!!
-CLIK!-
AWW! CREEPER THANK WOLF AND SPIDER!
YOU'RE WELCOME, BUD. WE'LL COME BY TOMORROW, SEE HOW YOU'RE DOING, OKAY?
NOD!

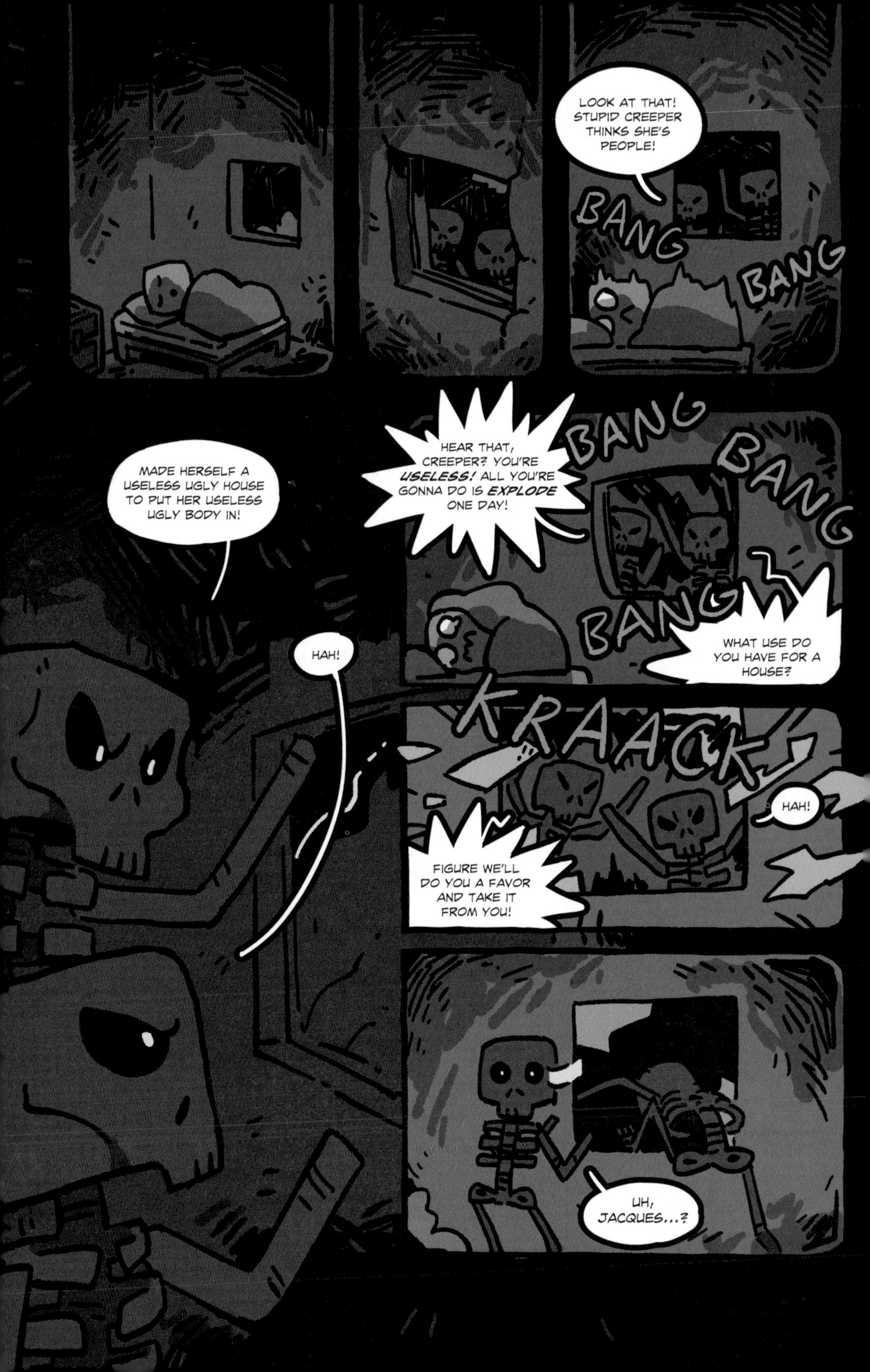
LOOK AT THAT! STUPID CREEPER THINKS SHE'S PEOPLE!
BANG
BANG
MADE HERSELF A USELESS UGLY HOUSE TO PUT HER USELESS UGLY BODY IN!
HEAR THAT, CREEPER? YOU'RE *USELESS!* ALL YOU'RE GONNA DO IS *EXPLODE* ONE DAY!
BANG
BANG
BANG
WHAT USE DO YOU HAVE FOR A HOUSE?
HAH!
KRAACK
HAH!
FIGURE WE'LL DO YOU A FAVOR AND TAKE IT FROM YOU!
UH, JACQUES...?

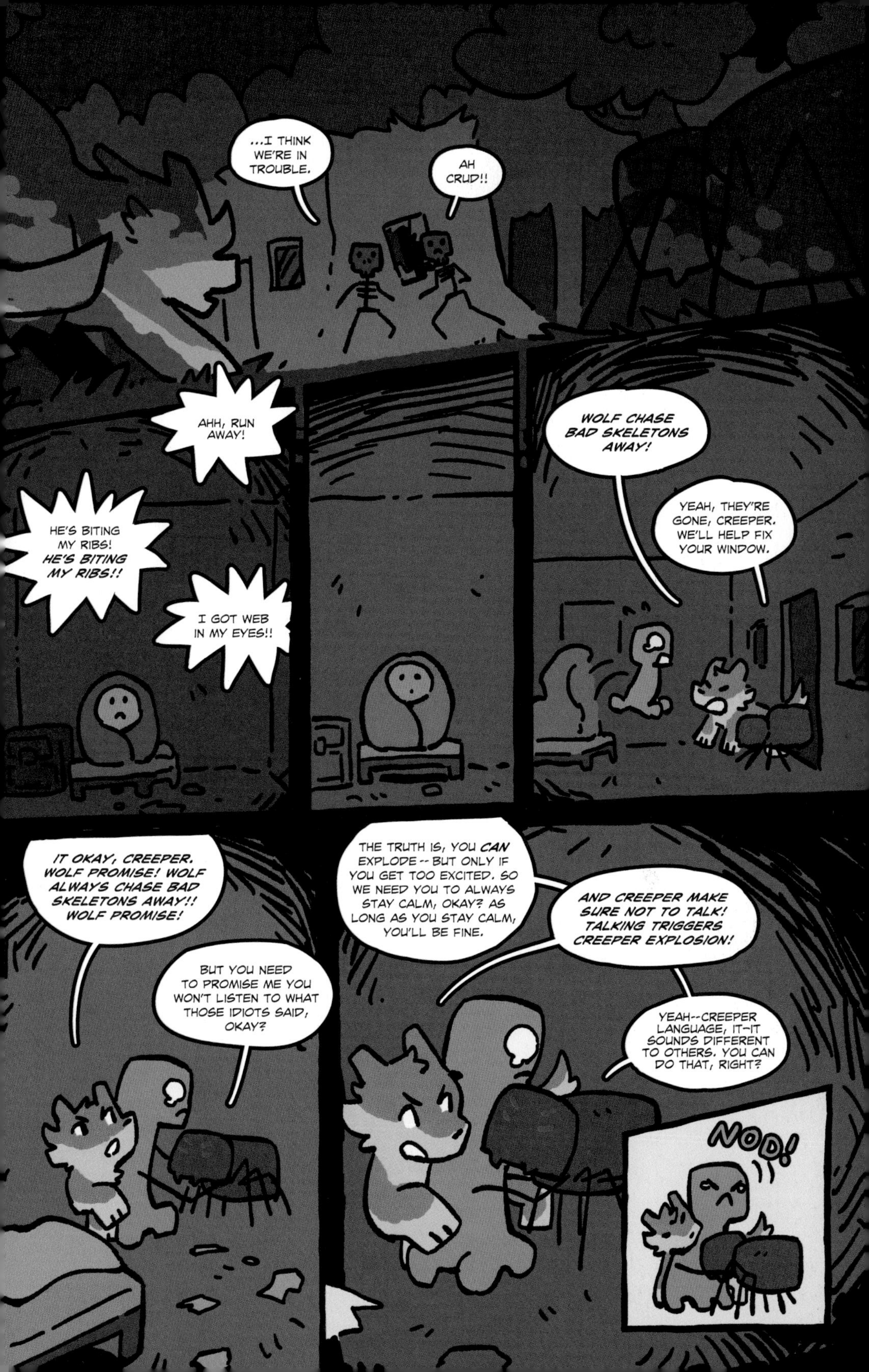
...I THINK WE'RE IN TROUBLE.
AH CRUD!!
AHH, RUN AWAY!
HE'S BITING MY RIBS! *HE'S BITING MY RIBS!!*
I GOT WEB IN MY EYES!!
WOLF CHASE BAD SKELETONS AWAY!
YEAH, THEY'RE GONE, CREEPER. WE'LL HELP FIX YOUR WINDOW.
IT OKAY, CREEPER. WOLF PROMISE! WOLF ALWAYS CHASE BAD SKELETONS AWAY!! WOLF PROMISE!
BUT YOU NEED TO PROMISE ME YOU WON'T LISTEN TO WHAT THOSE IDIOTS SAID, OKAY?
THE TRUTH IS, YOU *CAN* EXPLODE -- BUT ONLY IF YOU GET TOO EXCITED. SO WE NEED YOU TO ALWAYS STAY CALM, OKAY? AS LONG AS YOU STAY CALM, YOU'LL BE FINE.
AND CREEPER MAKE SURE NOT TO TALK! TALKING TRIGGERS CREEPER EXPLOSION!
YEAH--CREEPER LANGUAGE, IT--IT SOUNDS DIFFERENT TO OTHERS. YOU CAN DO THAT, RIGHT?
NOD!

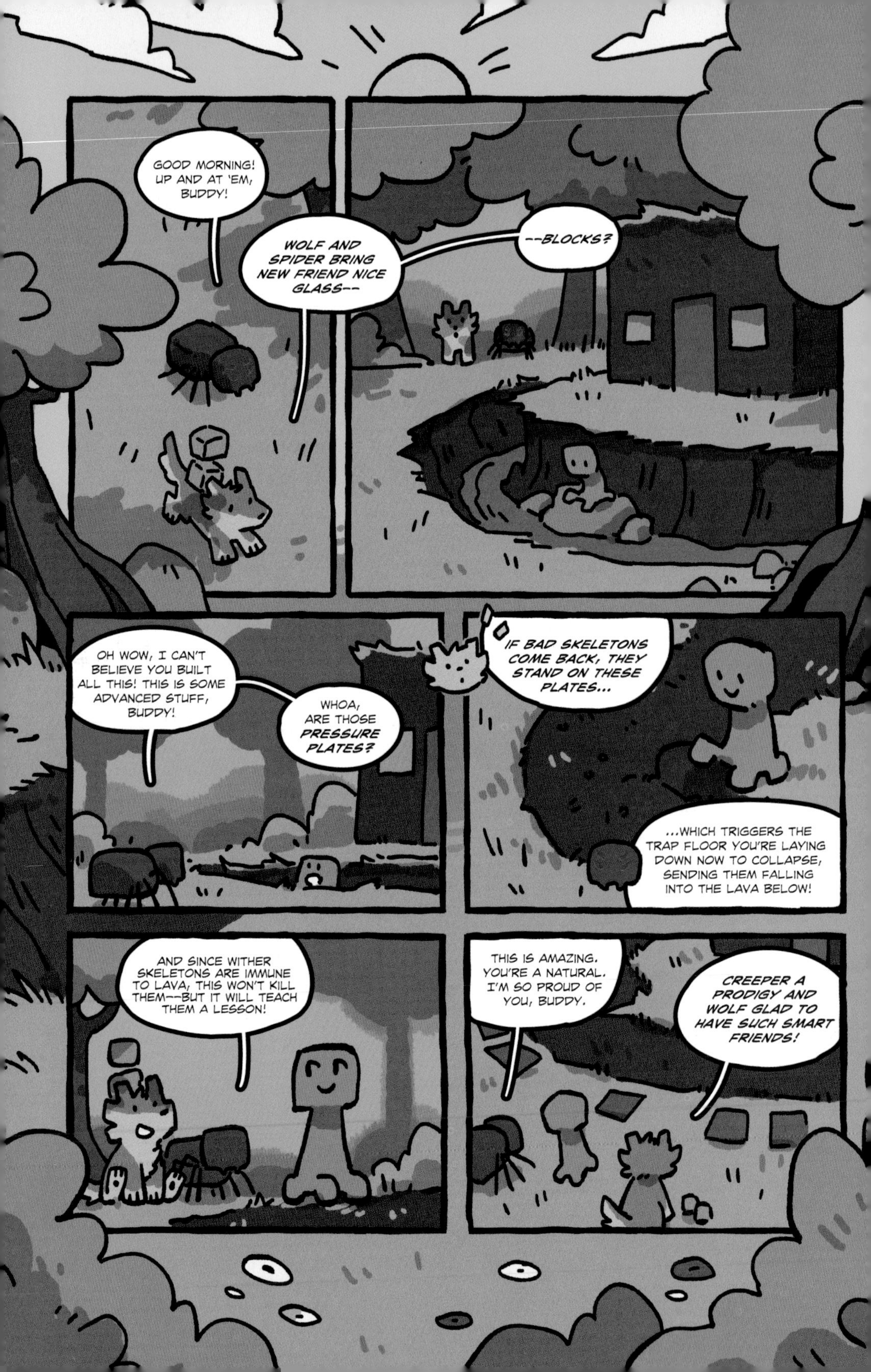
GOOD MORNING! UP AND AT 'EM, BUDDY!
WOLF AND SPIDER BRING NEW FRIEND NICE GLASS--
--BLOCKS?
OH WOW, I CAN'T BELIEVE YOU BUILT ALL THIS! THIS IS SOME ADVANCED STUFF, BUDDY!
WHOA, ARE THOSE PRESSURE PLATES?
IF BAD SKELETONS COME BACK, THEY STAND ON THESE PLATES...
...WHICH TRIGGERS THE TRAP FLOOR YOU'RE LAYING DOWN NOW TO COLLAPSE, SENDING THEM FALLING INTO THE LAVA BELOW!
AND SINCE WITHER SKELETONS ARE IMMUNE TO LAVA, THIS WON'T KILL THEM--BUT IT WILL TEACH THEM A LESSON!
THIS IS AMAZING. YOU'RE A NATURAL. I'M SO PROUD OF YOU, BUDDY.
CREEPER A PRODIGY AND WOLF GLAD TO HAVE SUCH SMART FRIENDS!

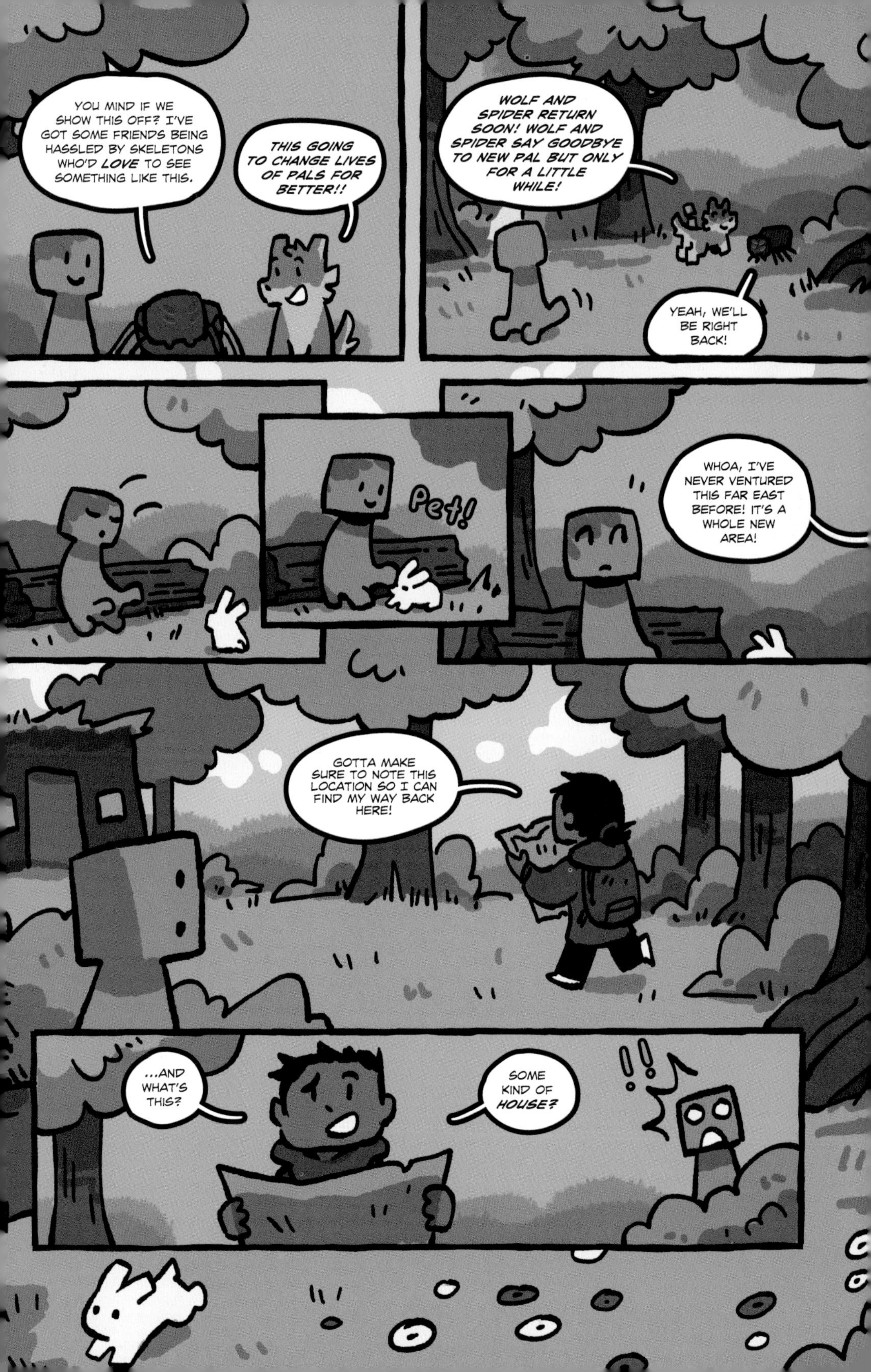
YOU MIND IF WE SHOW THIS OFF? I'VE GOT SOME FRIENDS BEING HASSLED BY SKELETONS WHO'D LOVE TO SEE SOMETHING LIKE THIS.
THIS GOING TO CHANGE LIVES OF PALS FOR BETTER!!
WOLF AND SPIDER RETURN SOON! WOLF AND SPIDER SAY GOODBYE TO NEW PAL BUT ONLY FOR A LITTLE WHILE!
YEAH, WE'LL BE RIGHT BACK!
Pet!
WHOA, I'VE NEVER VENTURED THIS FAR EAST BEFORE! IT'S A WHOLE NEW AREA!
GOTTA MAKE SURE TO NOTE THIS LOCATION SO I CAN FIND MY WAY BACK HERE!
...AND WHAT'S THIS?
SOME KIND OF HOUSE?
!!

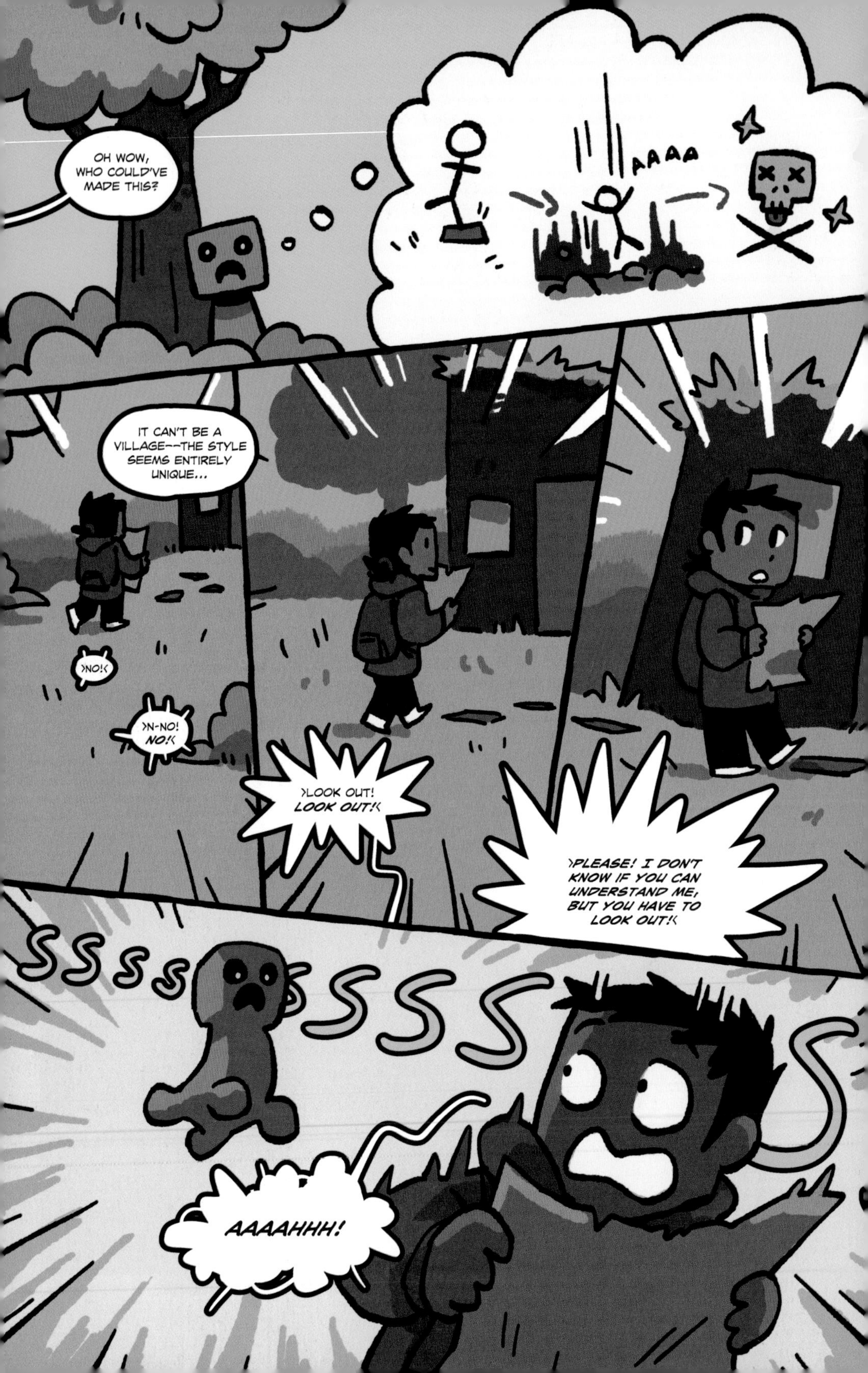

OH WOW, WHO COULD'VE MADE THIS?
AAAA
IT CAN'T BE A VILLAGE--THE STYLE SEEMS ENTIRELY UNIQUE...
›NO!‹
›N-NO! NO!‹
›LOOK OUT! LOOK OUT!‹
›PLEASE! I DON'T KNOW IF YOU CAN UNDERSTAND ME, BUT YOU HAVE TO LOOK OUT!‹
SSSSSSSSS
AAAAHHH!

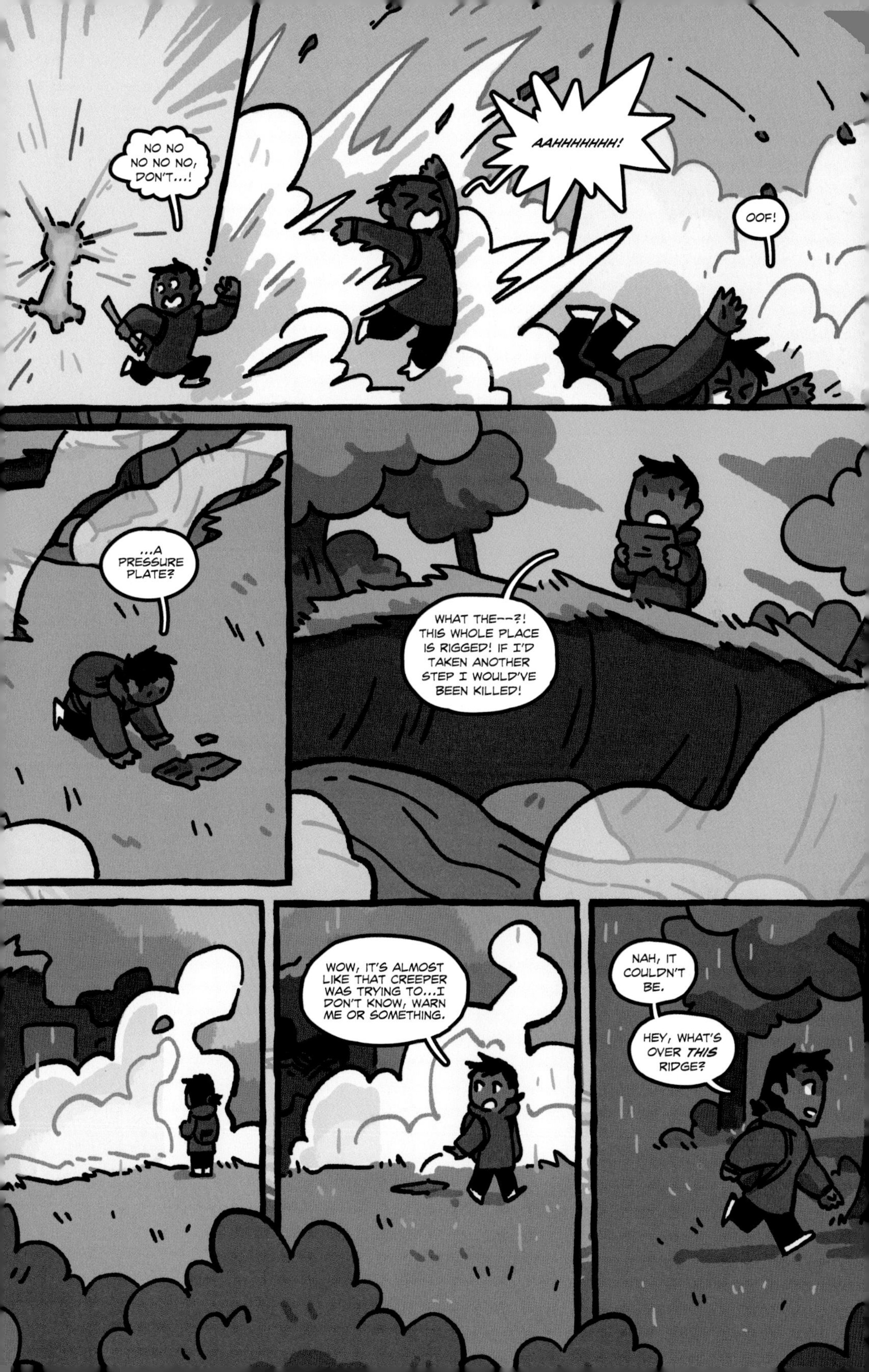
NO NO NO NO NO, DON'T...!
AAHHHHHHH!
OOF!
...A PRESSURE PLATE?
WHAT THE--?! THIS WHOLE PLACE IS RIGGED! IF I'D TAKEN ANOTHER STEP I WOULD'VE BEEN KILLED!
WOW, IT'S ALMOST LIKE THAT CREEPER WAS TRYING TO...I DON'T KNOW, WARN ME OR SOMETHING.
NAH, IT COULDN'T BE.
HEY, WHAT'S OVER *THIS* RIDGE?

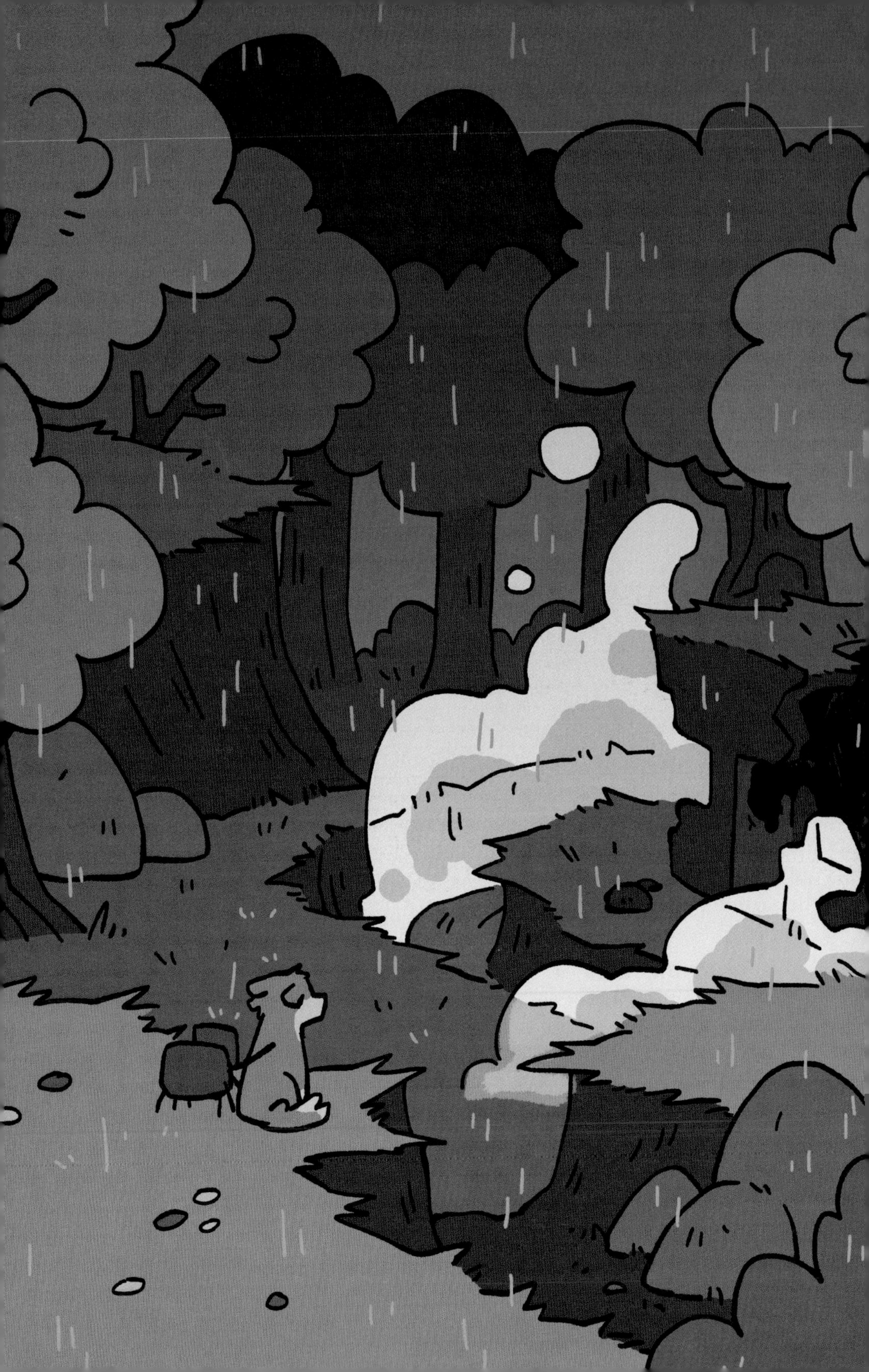

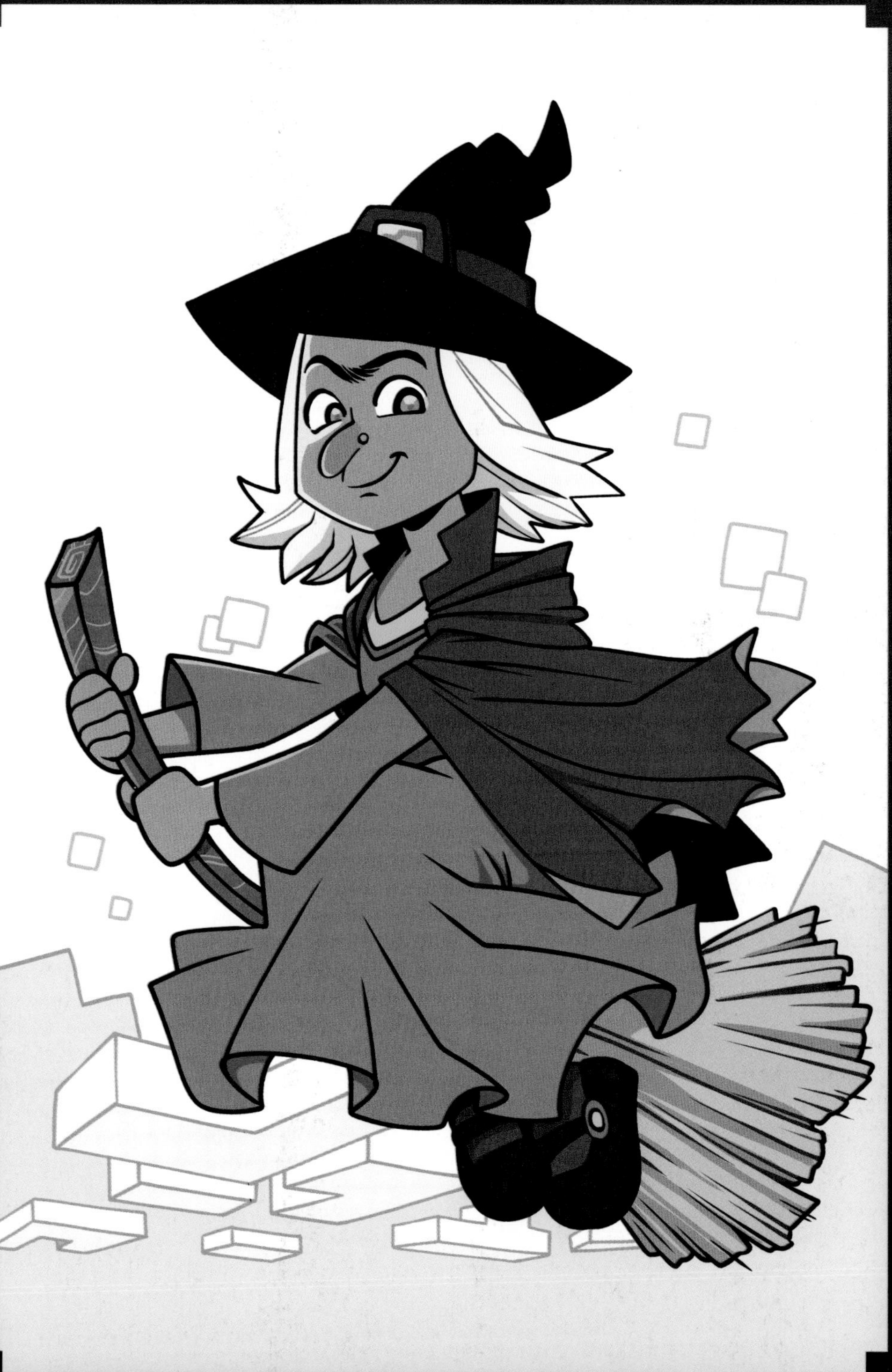

ILLUSTRATION BY

MADDI GONZALEZ

THE WITCH AND THE PILLAGER

STORY BY
RAFER ROBERTS

ART AND LETTERING BY
RYAN MANIULIT

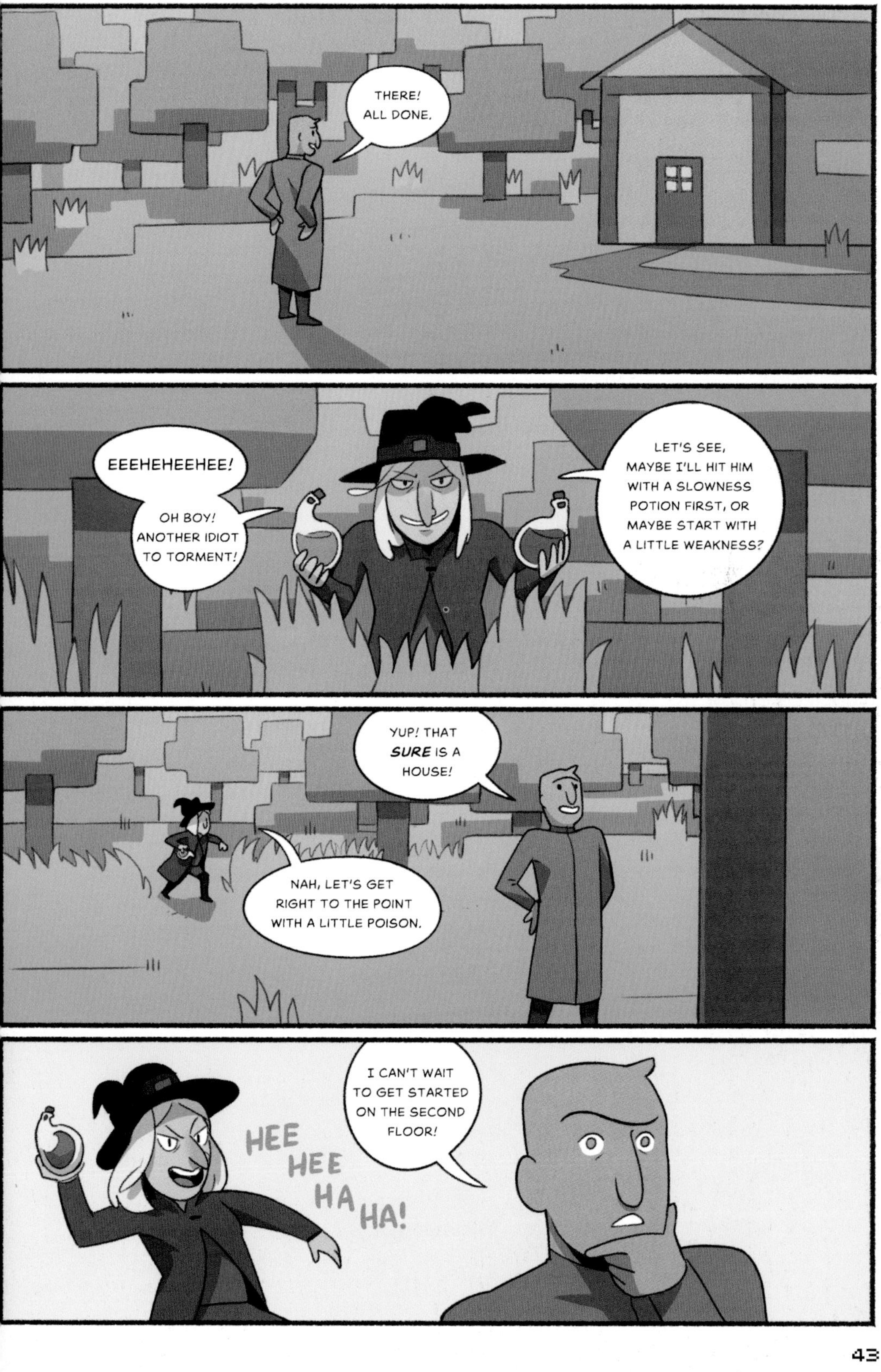
THERE! ALL DONE.
EEEHEHEEHEE!
OH BOY! ANOTHER IDIOT TO TORMENT!
LET'S SEE, MAYBE I'LL HIT HIM WITH A SLOWNESS POTION FIRST, OR MAYBE START WITH A LITTLE WEAKNESS?
YUP! THAT *SURE* IS A HOUSE!
NAH, LET'S GET RIGHT TO THE POINT WITH A LITTLE POISON.
I CAN'T WAIT TO GET STARTED ON THE SECOND FLOOR!
HEE HEE HA HA!

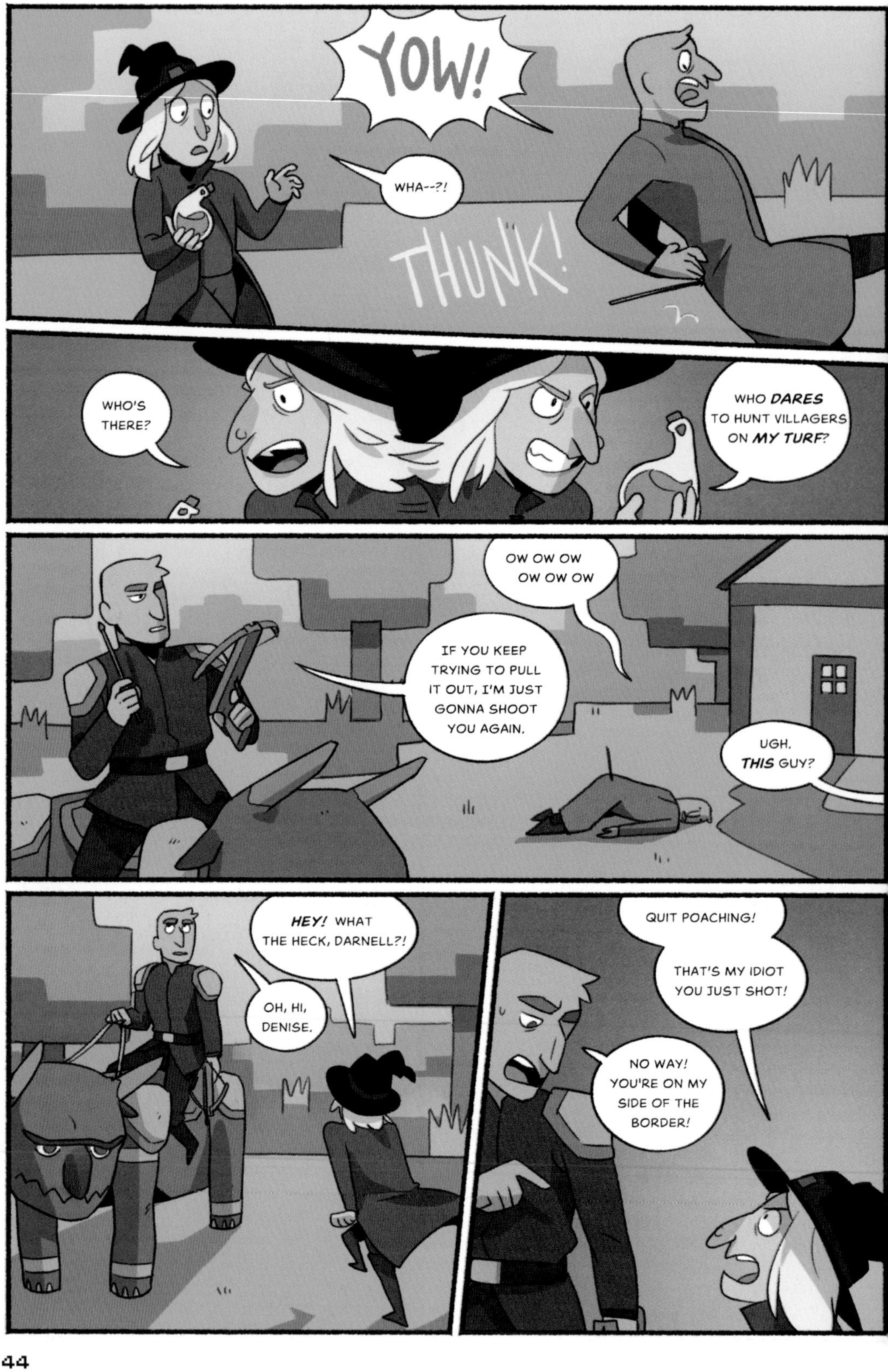
YOW!
WHA--?!
THUNK!
WHO'S THERE?
WHO **DARES** TO HUNT VILLAGERS ON ***MY TURF***?
OW OW OW OW OW OW
IF YOU KEEP TRYING TO PULL IT OUT, I'M JUST GONNA SHOOT YOU AGAIN.
UGH. **THIS** GUY?
HEY! WHAT THE HECK, DARNELL?!
OH, HI, DENISE.
QUIT POACHING!
THAT'S MY IDIOT YOU JUST SHOT!
NO WAY! YOU'RE ON MY SIDE OF THE BORDER!

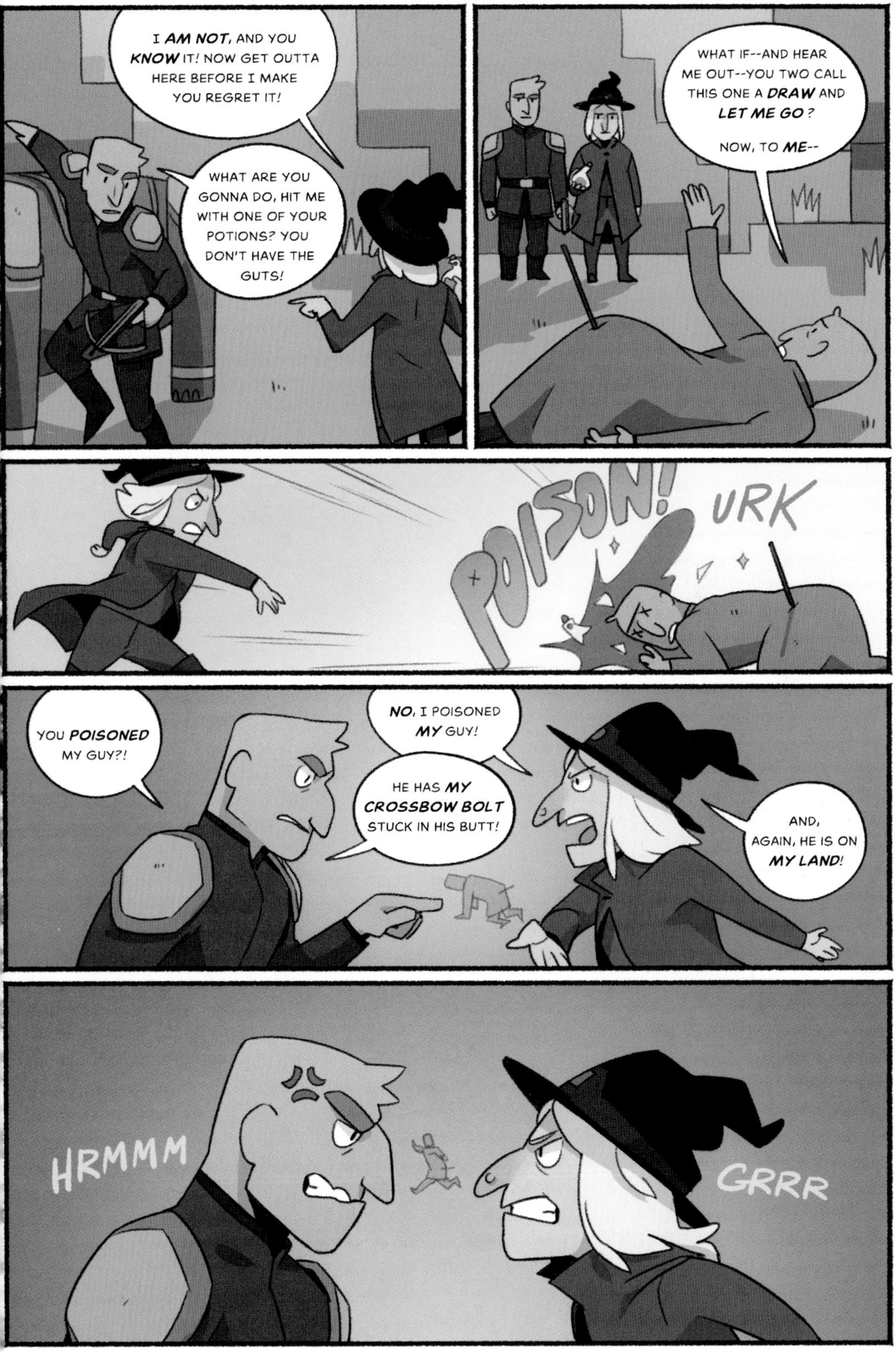
I AM NOT, AND YOU KNOW IT! NOW GET OUTTA HERE BEFORE I MAKE YOU REGRET IT!
WHAT ARE YOU GONNA DO, HIT ME WITH ONE OF YOUR POTIONS? YOU DON'T HAVE THE GUTS!
WHAT IF--AND HEAR ME OUT--YOU TWO CALL THIS ONE A DRAW AND LET ME GO?
NOW, TO ME--
POISON!
URK
YOU POISONED MY GUY?!
NO, I POISONED MY GUY!
HE HAS MY CROSSBOW BOLT STUCK IN HIS BUTT!
AND, AGAIN, HE IS ON MY LAND!
HRMMM
GRRR

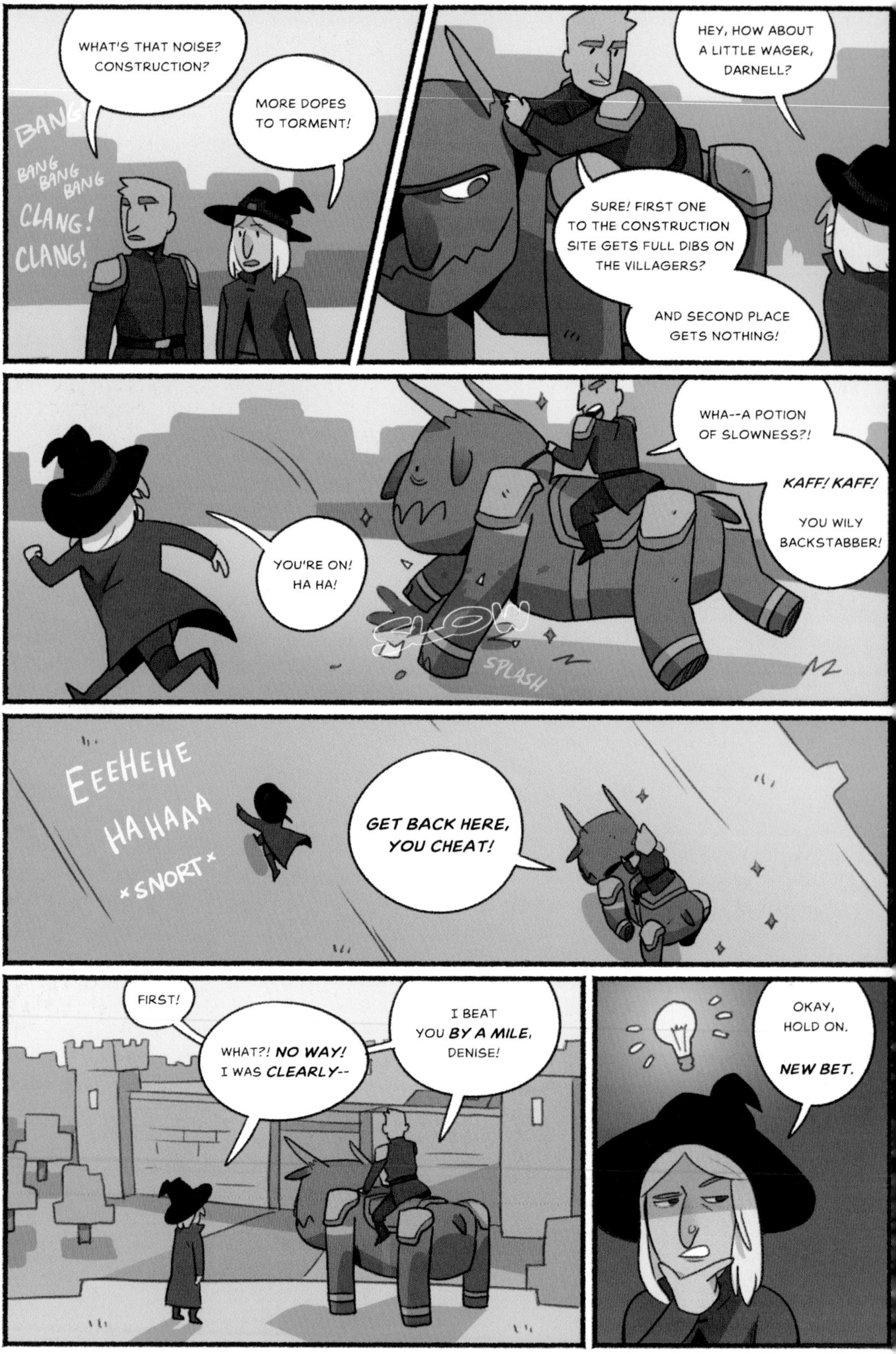

BANG
BANG BANG BANG
CLANG! CLANG!
WHAT'S THAT NOISE? CONSTRUCTION?
MORE DOPES TO TORMENT!
HEY, HOW ABOUT A LITTLE WAGER, DARNELL?
SURE! FIRST ONE TO THE CONSTRUCTION SITE GETS FULL DIBS ON THE VILLAGERS?
AND SECOND PLACE GETS NOTHING!
YOU'RE ON! HA HA!
SLOW
SPLASH
WHA--A POTION OF SLOWNESS?!
KAFF! KAFF!
YOU WILY BACKSTABBER!
EEEHEHE HAHAAA
×SNORT×
GET BACK HERE, YOU CHEAT!
FIRST!
WHAT?! NO WAY! I WAS CLEARLY--
I BEAT YOU BY A MILE, DENISE!
OKAY, HOLD ON. NEW BET.

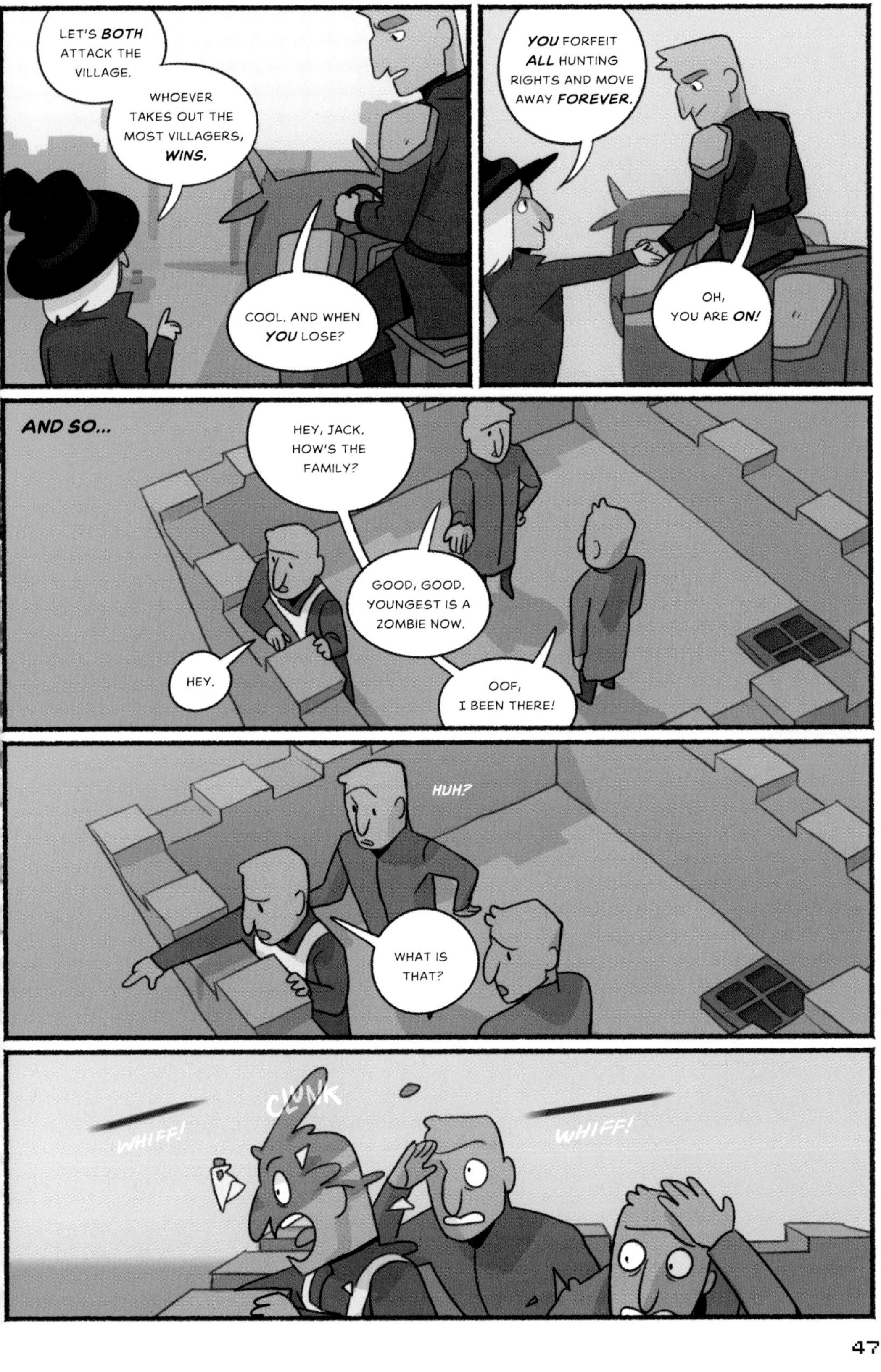
LET'S **BOTH** ATTACK THE VILLAGE.
WHOEVER TAKES OUT THE MOST VILLAGERS, **WINS.**
COOL. AND WHEN **YOU** LOSE?
YOU FORFEIT **ALL** HUNTING RIGHTS AND MOVE AWAY **FOREVER.**
OH, YOU ARE **ON!**
AND SO...
HEY, JACK. HOW'S THE FAMILY?
HEY.
GOOD, GOOD. YOUNGEST IS A ZOMBIE NOW.
OOF, I BEEN THERE!
HUH?
WHAT IS THAT?
WHIFF!
CLUNK
WHIFF!

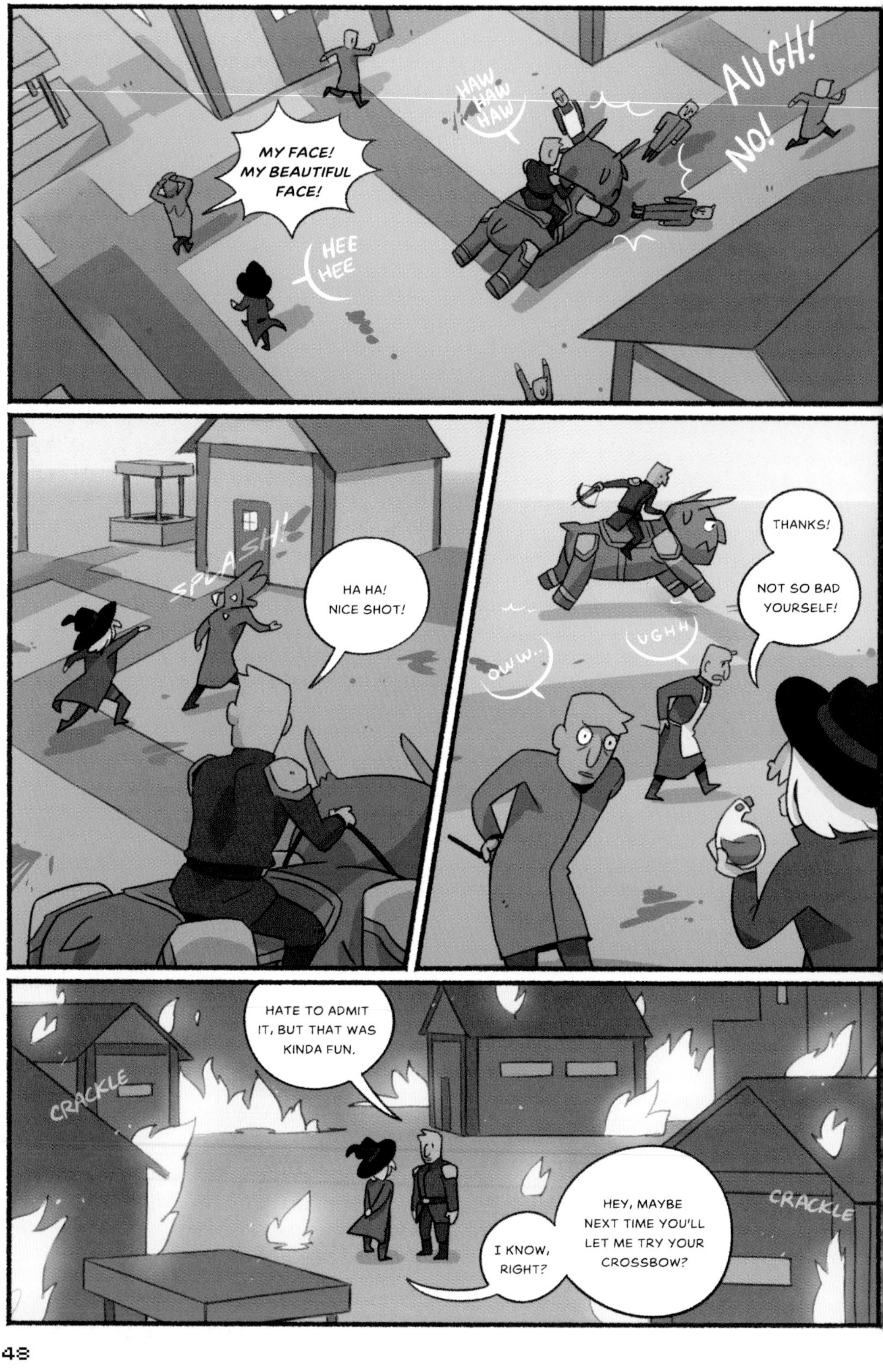

MY FACE! MY BEAUTIFUL FACE!
HAW HAW HAW
AUGH!
NO!
HEE HEE
SPLASH!
HA HA! NICE SHOT!
THANKS!
NOT SO BAD YOURSELF!
UGHH
OWW..
HATE TO ADMIT IT, BUT THAT WAS KINDA FUN.
CRACKLE
I KNOW, RIGHT?
HEY, MAYBE NEXT TIME YOU'LL LET ME TRY YOUR CROSSBOW?
CRACKLE

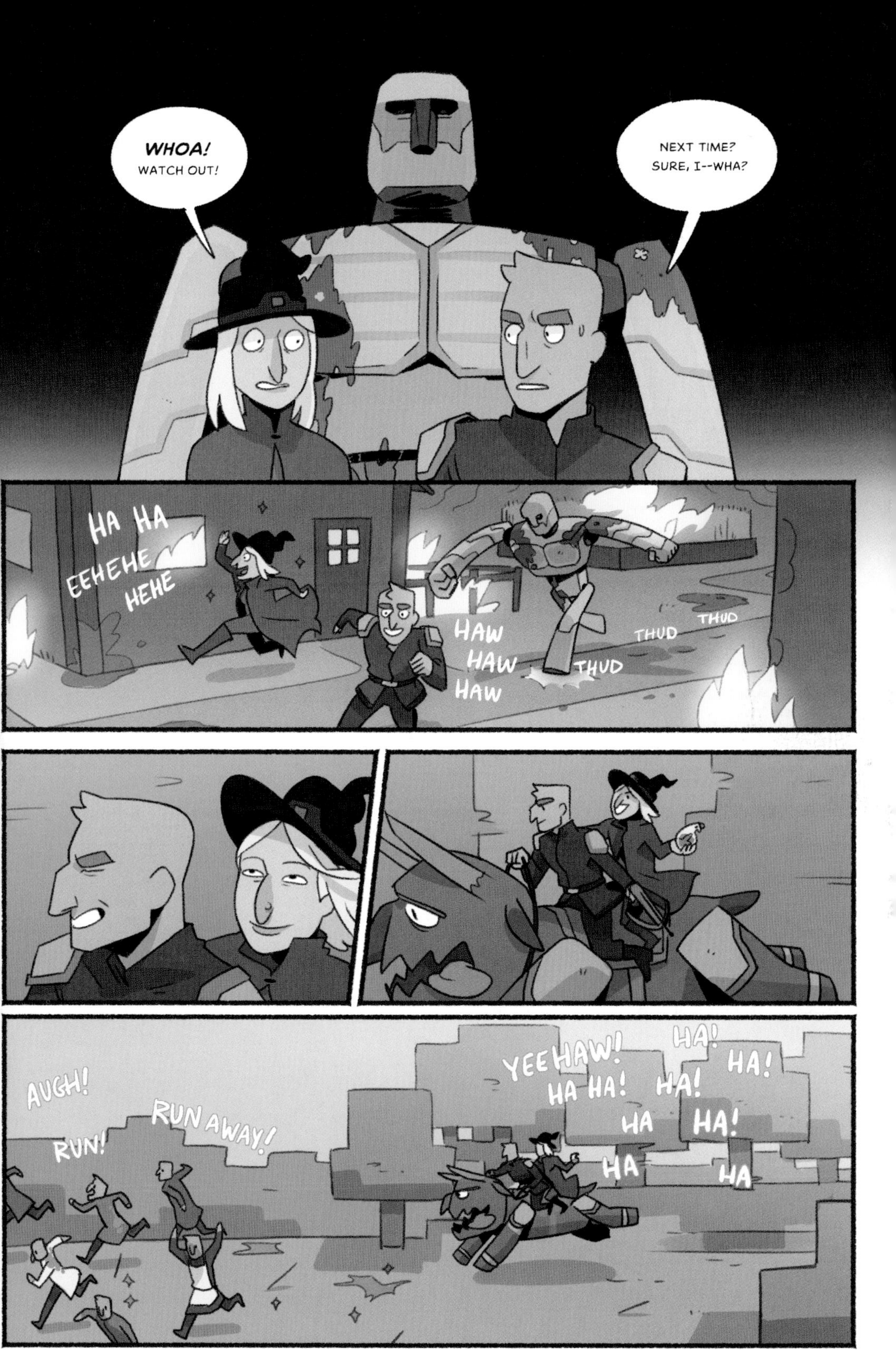
WHOA!
WATCH OUT!
NEXT TIME?
SURE, I--WHA?
HA HA
EEHEHE
HEHE
HAW
HAW
HAW
THUD
THUD
THUD
AUGH!
RUN!
RUN AWAY!
YEEHAW!
HA!
HA!
HA HA!
HA!
HA
HA!
HA
HA

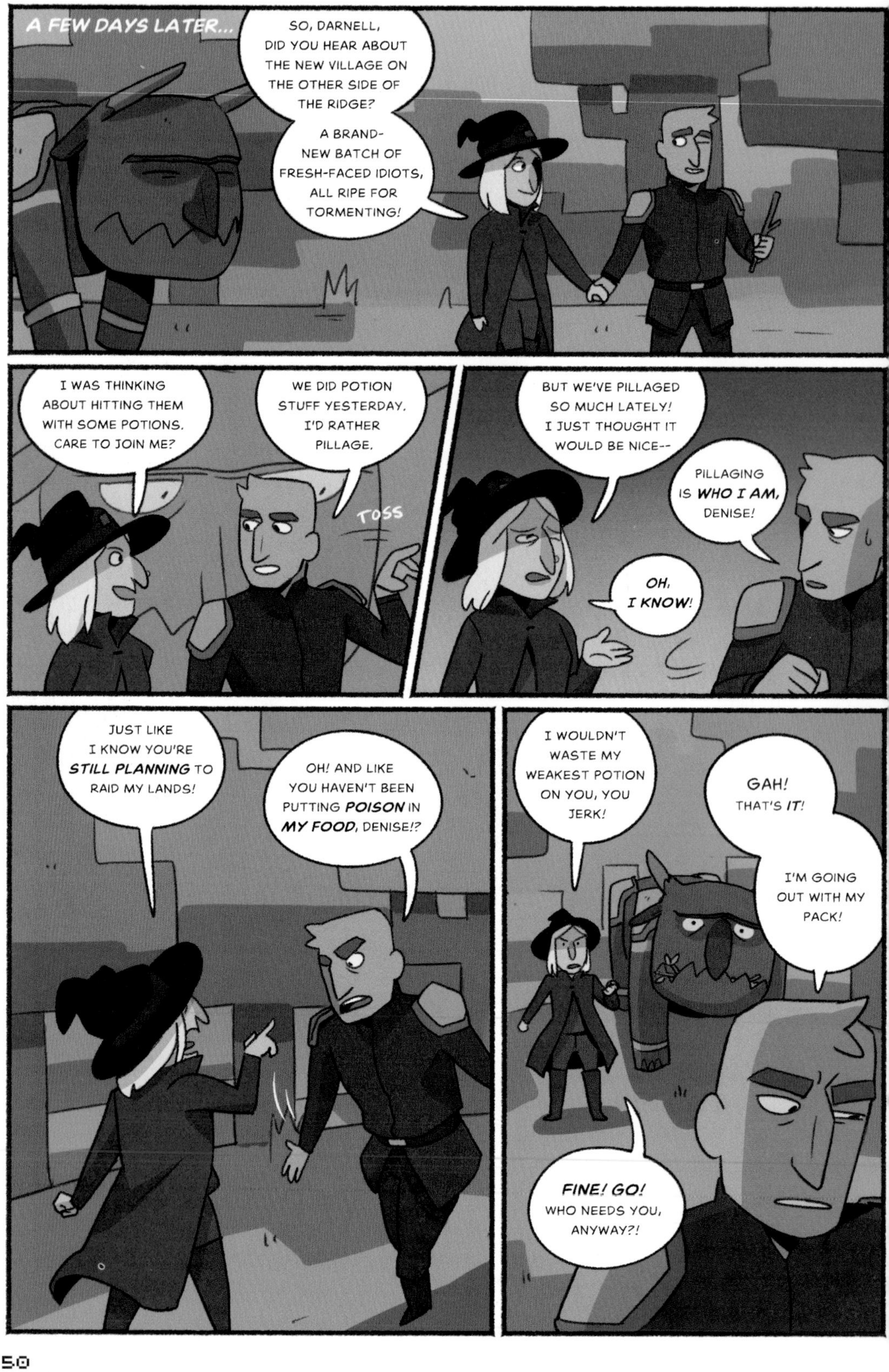
A FEW DAYS LATER...
SO, DARNELL, DID YOU HEAR ABOUT THE NEW VILLAGE ON THE OTHER SIDE OF THE RIDGE?
A BRAND-NEW BATCH OF FRESH-FACED IDIOTS, ALL RIPE FOR TORMENTING!
I WAS THINKING ABOUT HITTING THEM WITH SOME POTIONS. CARE TO JOIN ME?
WE DID POTION STUFF YESTERDAY. I'D RATHER PILLAGE.
TOSS
BUT WE'VE PILLAGED SO MUCH LATELY! I JUST THOUGHT IT WOULD BE NICE--
PILLAGING IS WHO I AM, DENISE!
OH, I KNOW!
JUST LIKE I KNOW YOU'RE STILL PLANNING TO RAID MY LANDS!
OH! AND LIKE YOU HAVEN'T BEEN PUTTING POISON IN MY FOOD, DENISE!?
I WOULDN'T WASTE MY WEAKEST POTION ON YOU, YOU JERK!
GAH! THAT'S IT!
I'M GOING OUT WITH MY PACK!
FINE! GO! WHO NEEDS YOU, ANYWAY?!

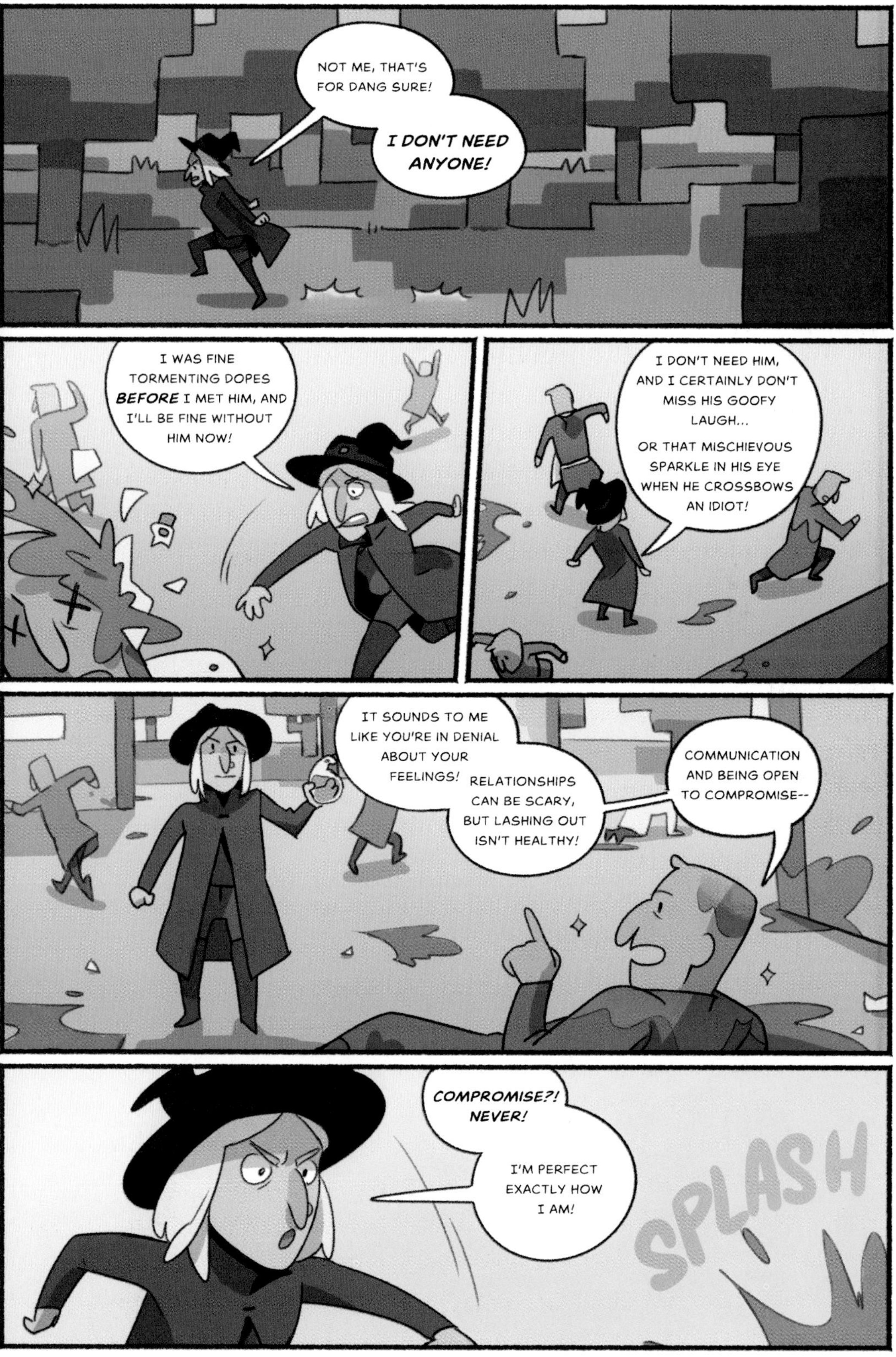
NOT ME, THAT'S FOR DANG SURE!
I DON'T NEED ANYONE!
I WAS FINE TORMENTING DOPES BEFORE I MET HIM, AND I'LL BE FINE WITHOUT HIM NOW!
I DON'T NEED HIM, AND I CERTAINLY DON'T MISS HIS GOOFY LAUGH...
OR THAT MISCHIEVOUS SPARKLE IN HIS EYE WHEN HE CROSSBOWS AN IDIOT!
IT SOUNDS TO ME LIKE YOU'RE IN DENIAL ABOUT YOUR FEELINGS!
RELATIONSHIPS CAN BE SCARY, BUT LASHING OUT ISN'T HEALTHY!
COMMUNICATION AND BEING OPEN TO COMPROMISE--
COMPROMISE?! NEVER!
I'M PERFECT EXACTLY HOW I AM!
SPLASH

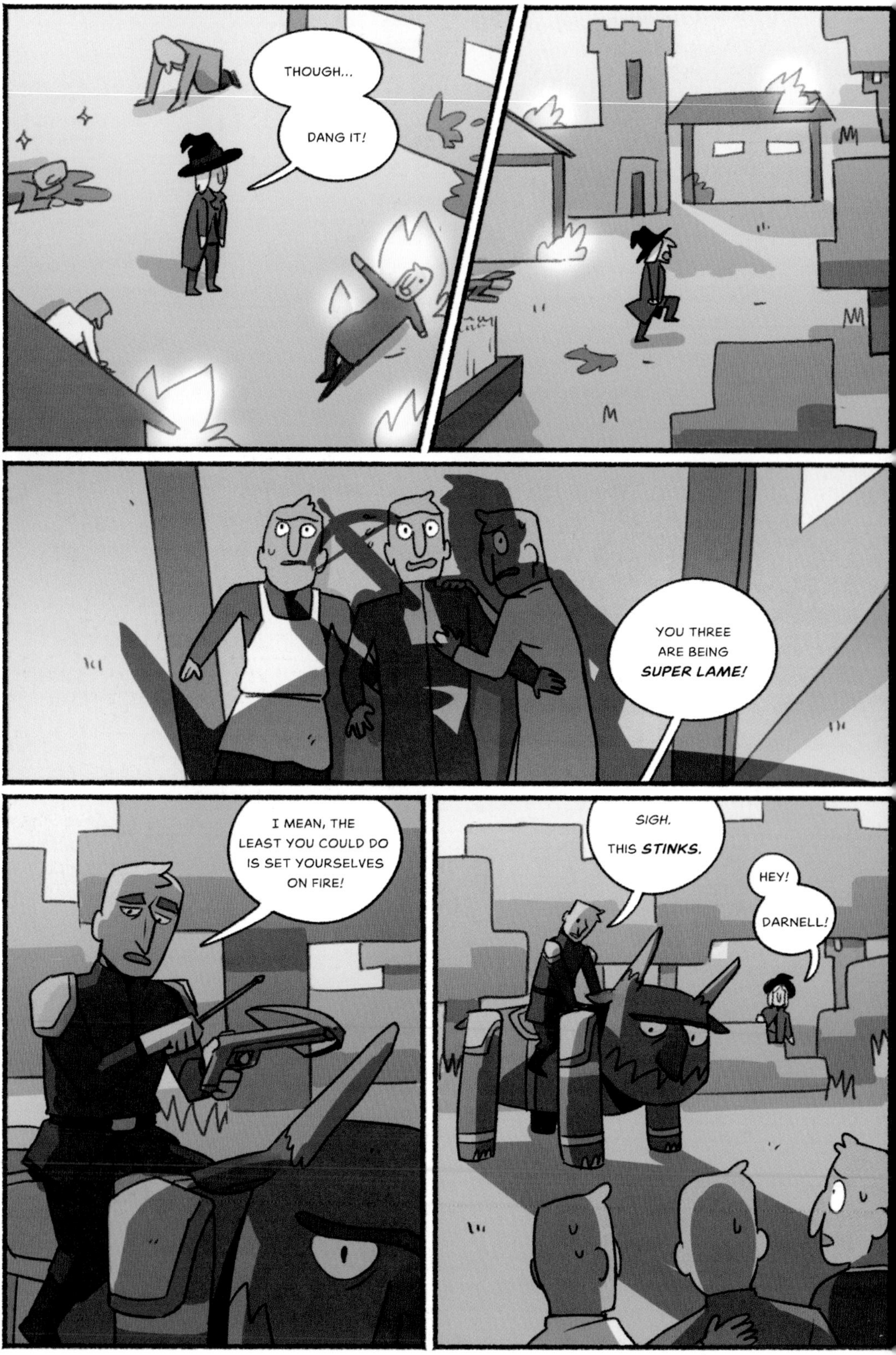
THOUGH...
DANG IT!
YOU THREE ARE BEING SUPER LAME!
I MEAN, THE LEAST YOU COULD DO IS SET YOURSELVES ON FIRE!
SIGH.
THIS STINKS.
HEY!
DARNELL!

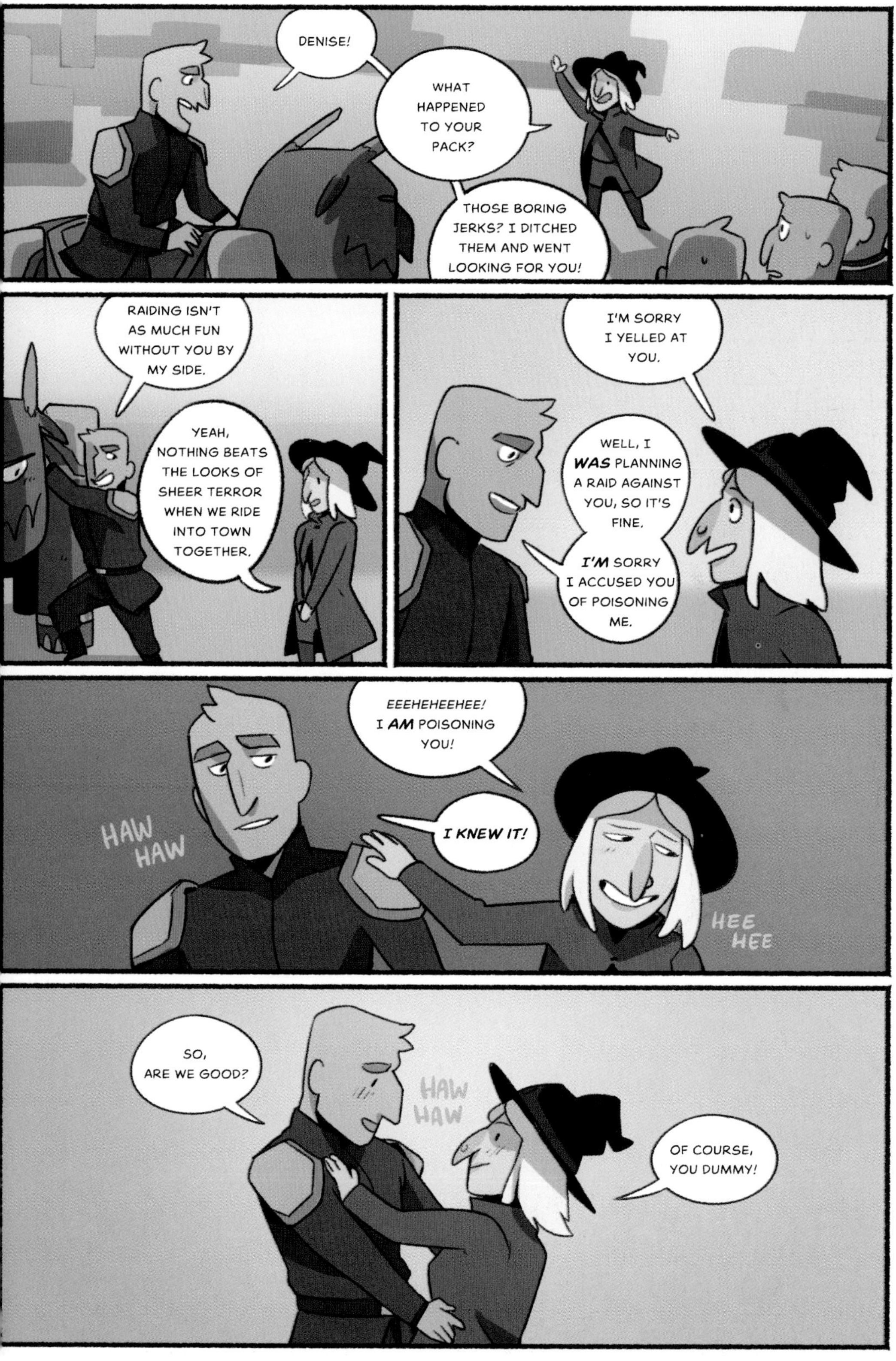
DENISE!
WHAT HAPPENED TO YOUR PACK?
THOSE BORING JERKS? I DITCHED THEM AND WENT LOOKING FOR YOU!
RAIDING ISN'T AS MUCH FUN WITHOUT YOU BY MY SIDE.
YEAH, NOTHING BEATS THE LOOKS OF SHEER TERROR WHEN WE RIDE INTO TOWN TOGETHER.
I'M SORRY I YELLED AT YOU.
WELL, I WAS PLANNING A RAID AGAINST YOU, SO IT'S FINE.
I'M SORRY I ACCUSED YOU OF POISONING ME.
EEEHEHEEHEE! I AM POISONING YOU!
I KNEW IT!
HAW HAW
HEE HEE
SO, ARE WE GOOD?
HAW HAW
OF COURSE, YOU DUMMY!

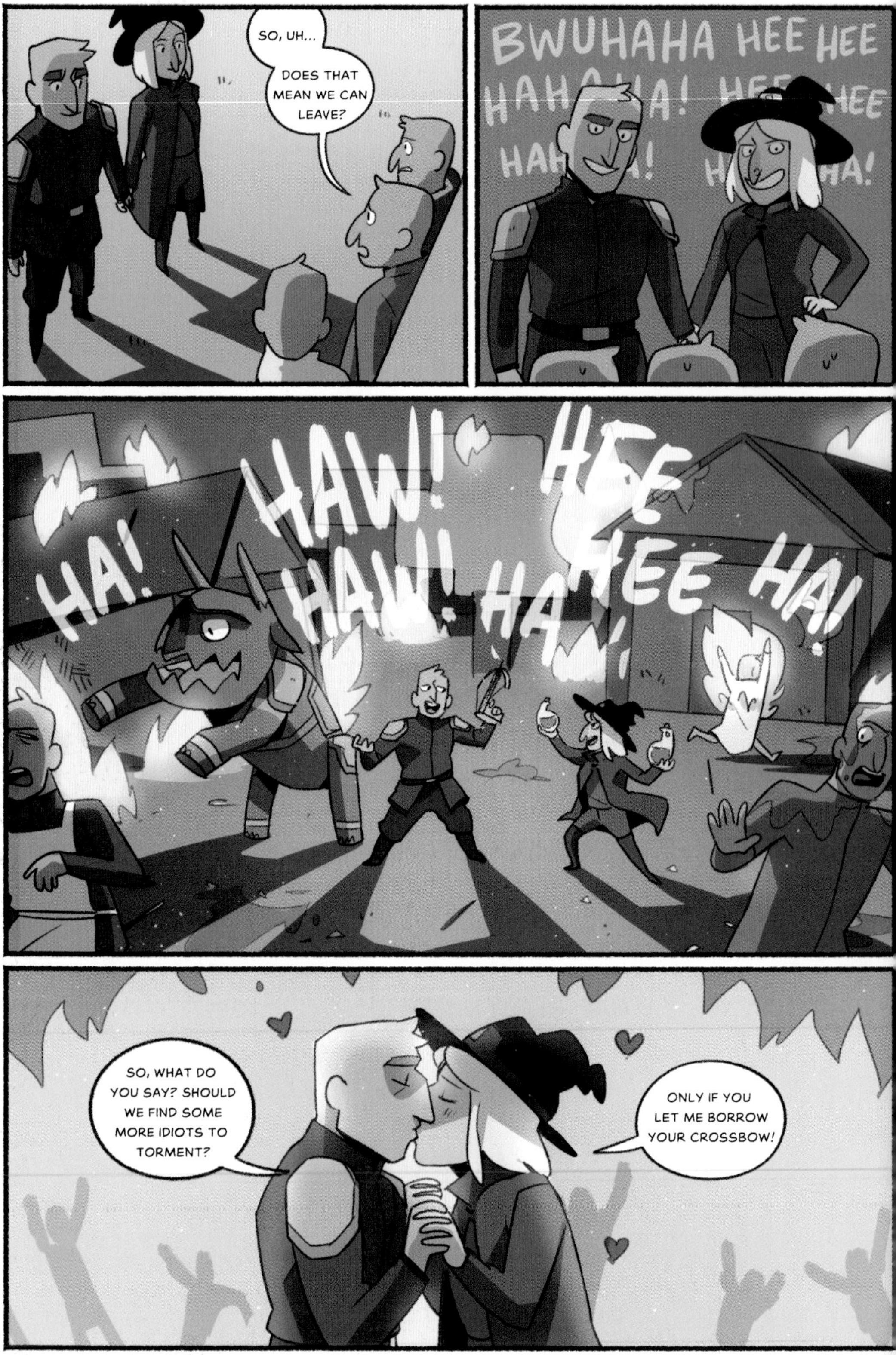
SO, UH...
DOES THAT MEAN WE CAN LEAVE?
BWUHAHA HEE HEE
HAHAHA! HEE HEE
HAHAHA! HAHAHA!
HA! HAW! HEE
HAW! HA HEE HA!
HAW!
SO, WHAT DO YOU SAY? SHOULD WE FIND SOME MORE IDIOTS TO TORMENT?
ONLY IF YOU LET ME BORROW YOUR CROSSBOW!

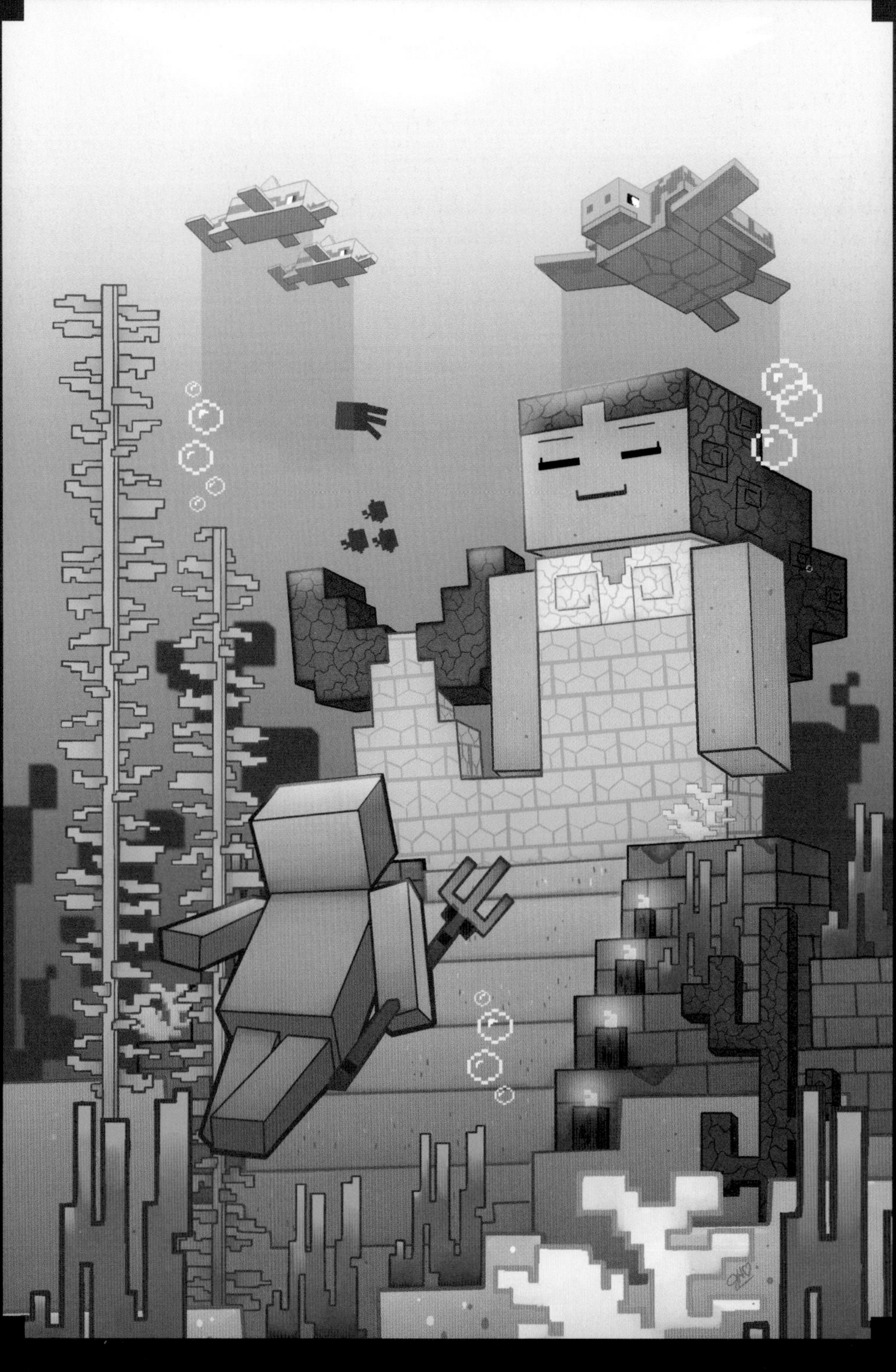

ILLUSTRATION BY

JENNIFER HERNANDEZ

A PIG'S TALE

STORY, ART, AND LETTERING BY
STEPHEN McCRANIE

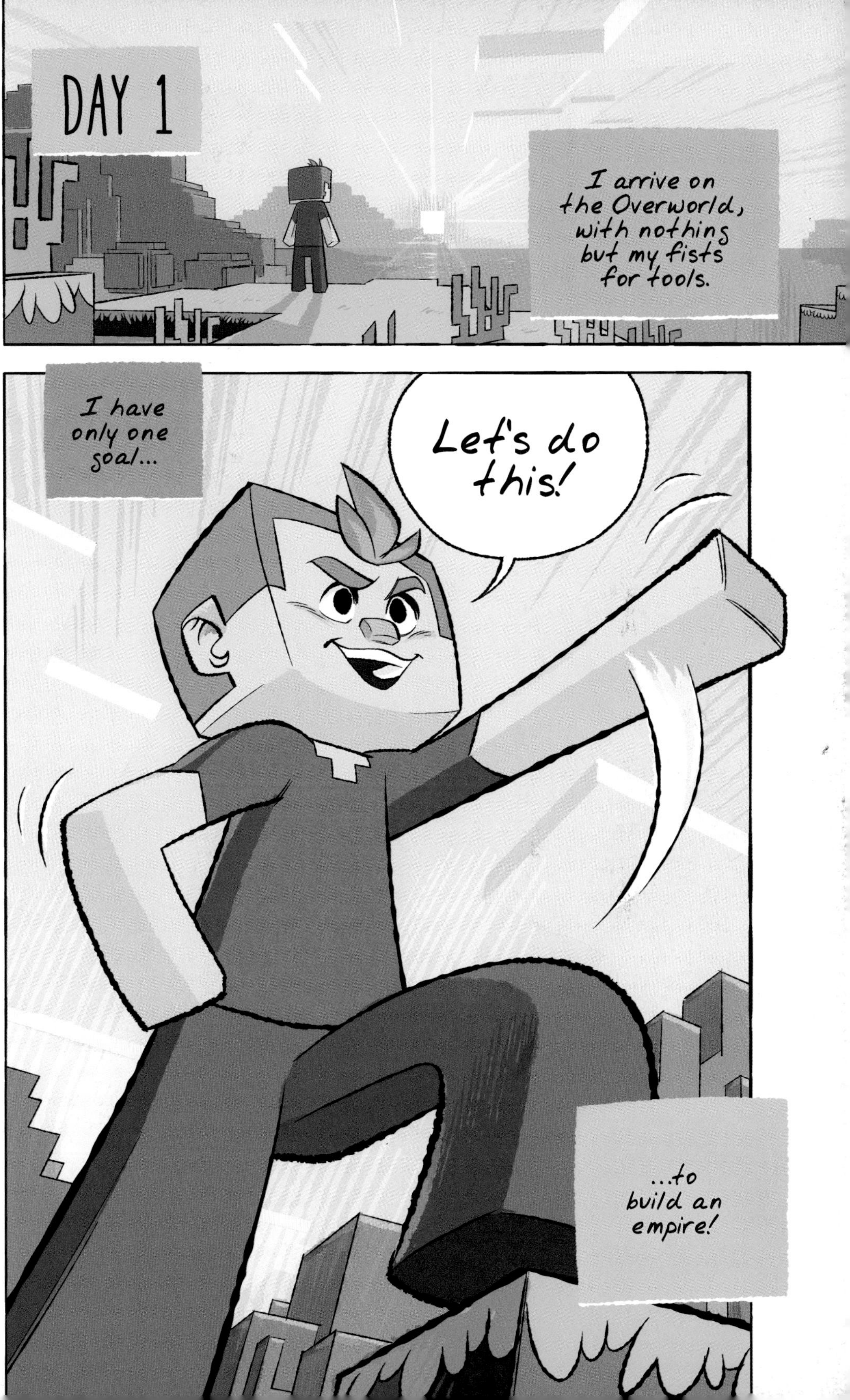
DAY 1
I arrive on the Overworld, with nothing but my fists for tools.
I have only one goal...
Let's do this!
...to build an empire!

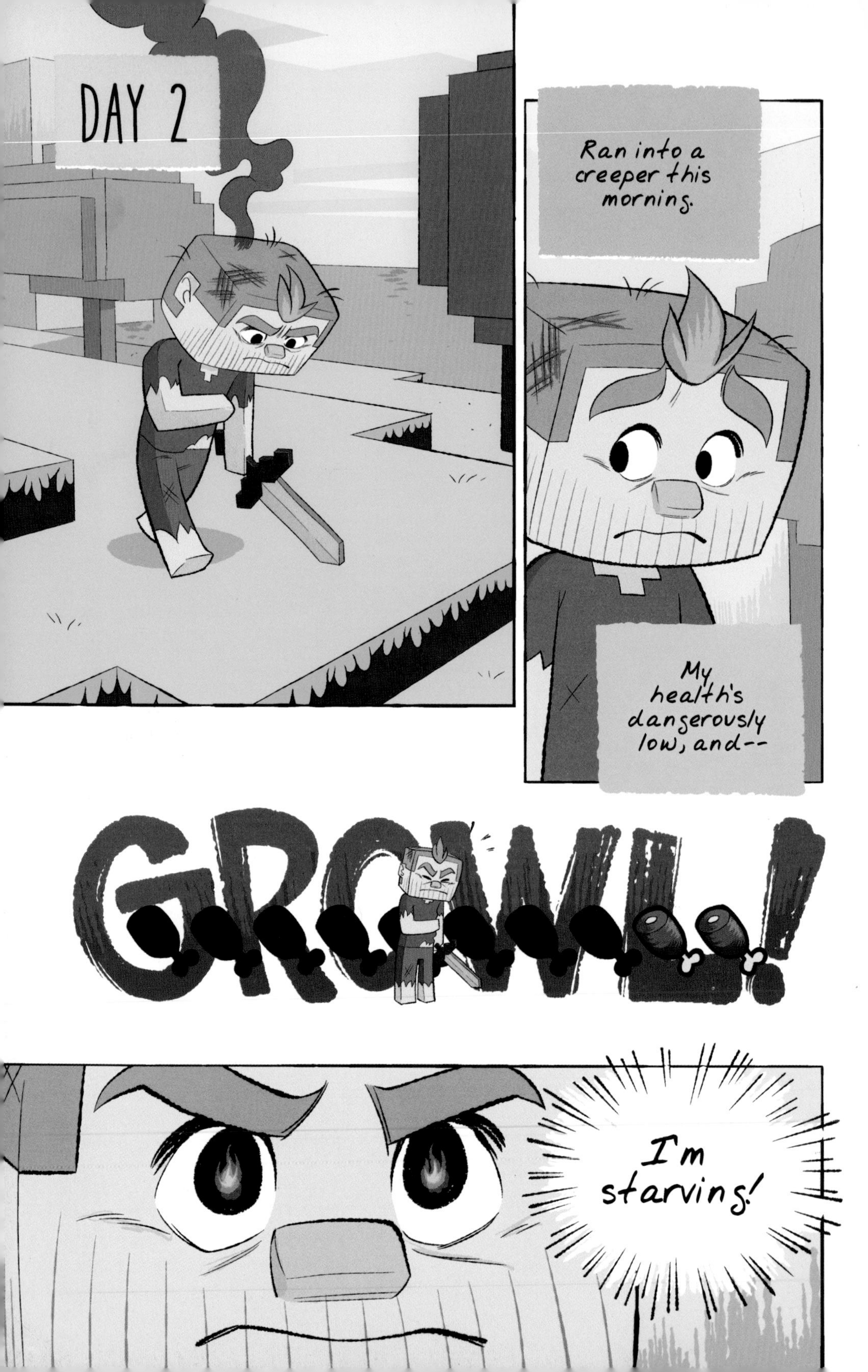
DAY 2
Ran into a creeper this morning.
My health's dangerously low, and--
GROWL!
I'm starving!

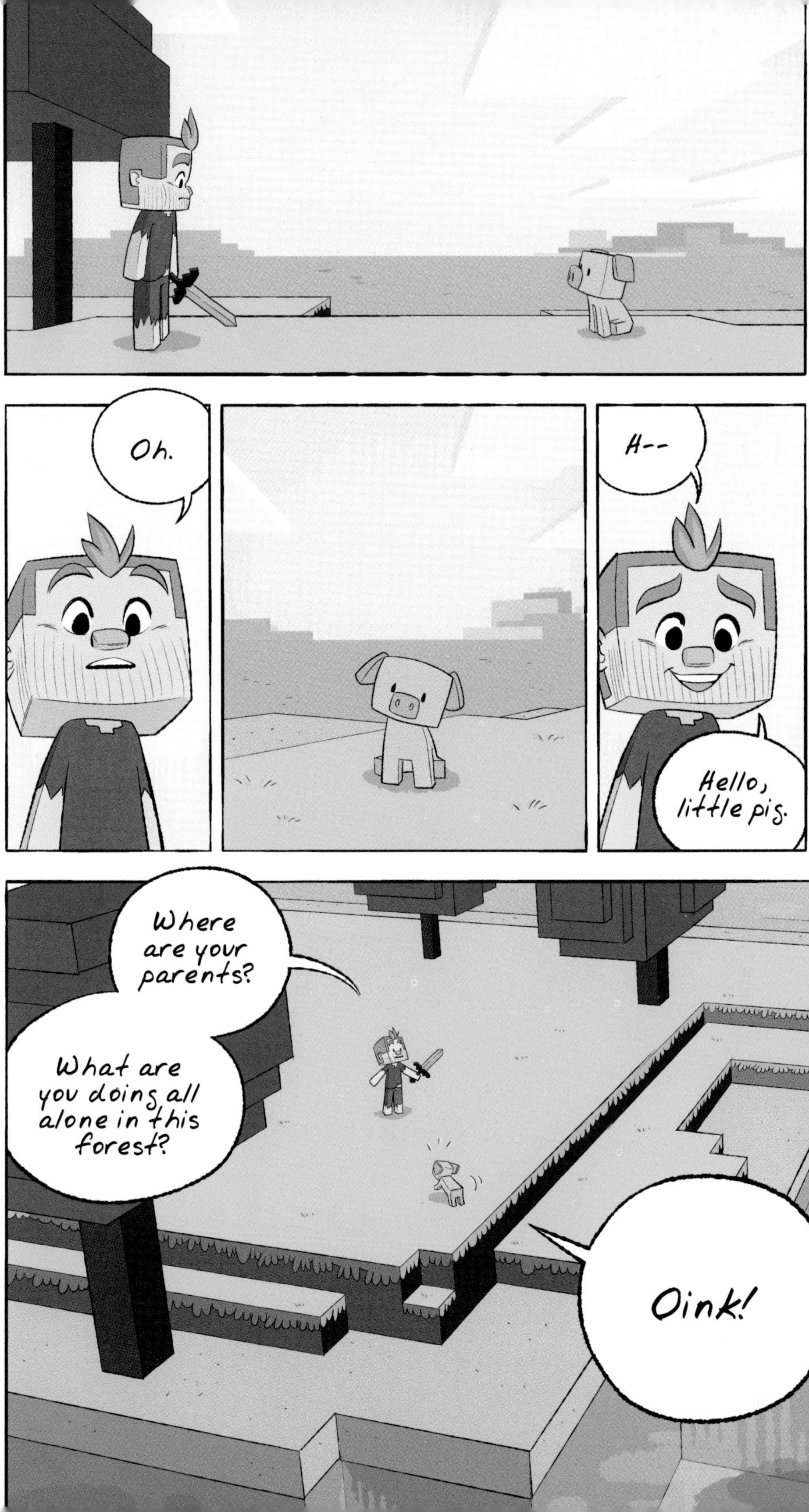

Oh.
H--
Hello, little pig.
Where are your parents?
What are you doing all alone in this forest?
Oink!

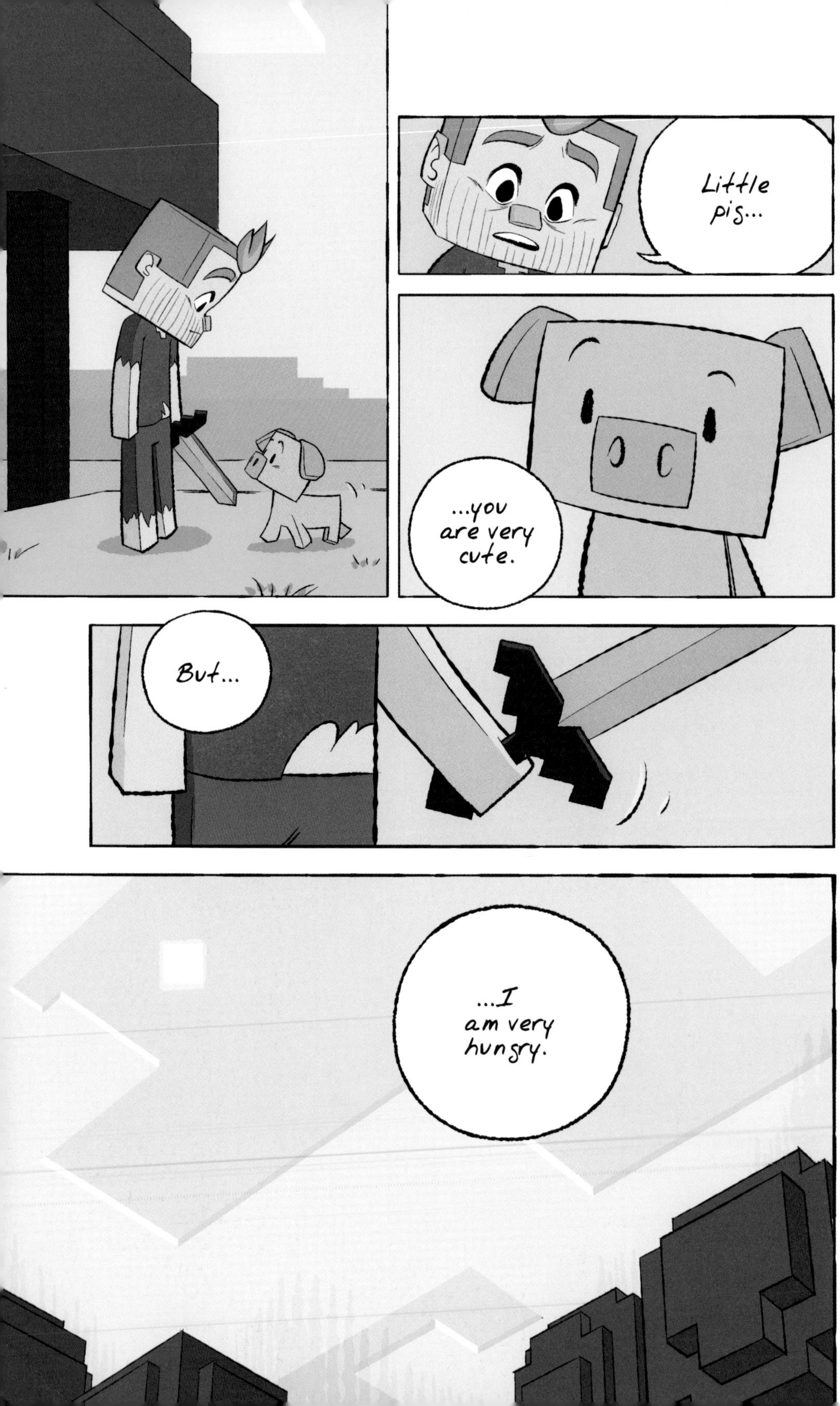
Little pig...
...you are very cute.
But...
...I am very hungry.

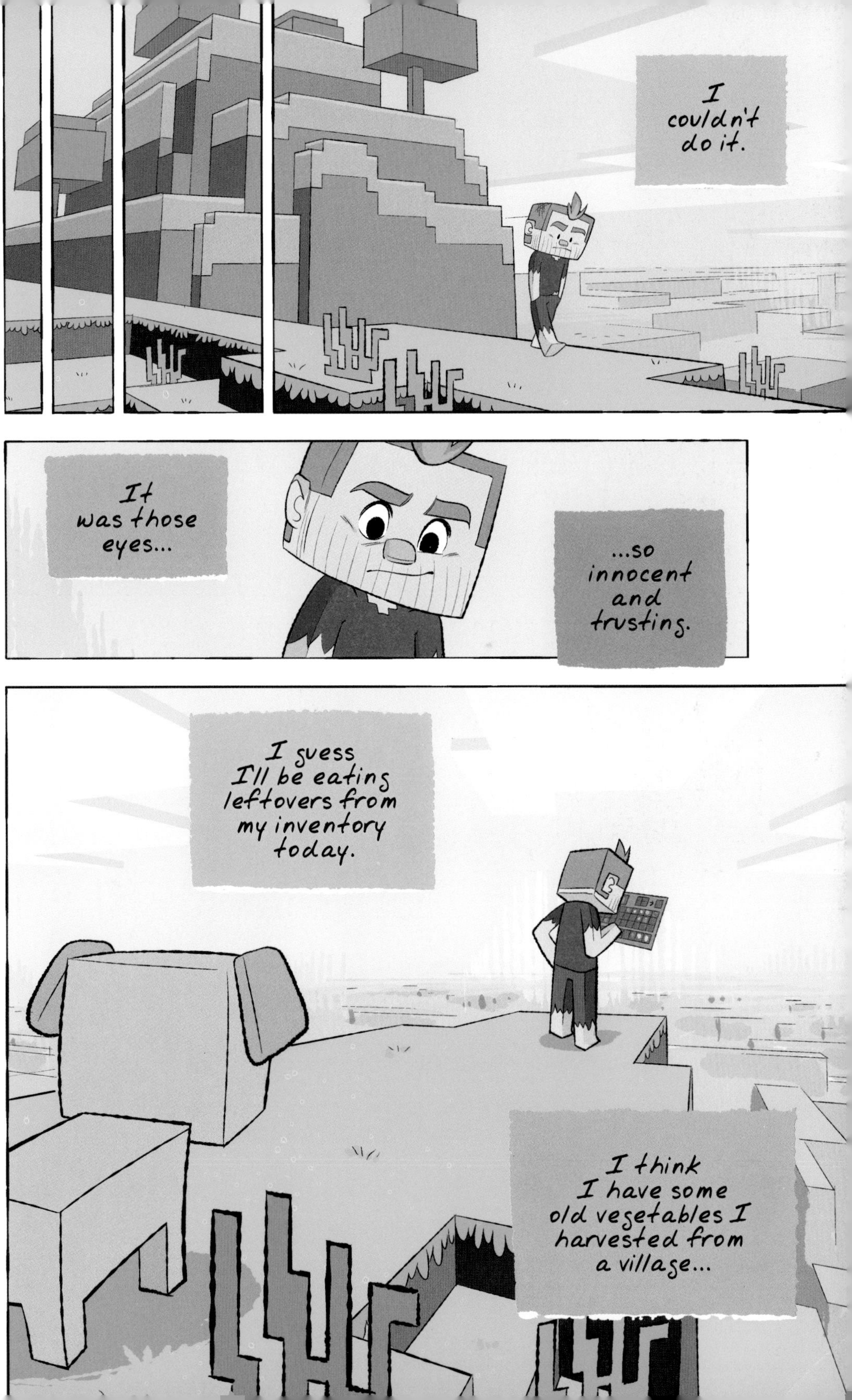
I couldn't do it.
It was those eyes...
...so innocent and trusting.
I guess I'll be eating leftovers from my inventory today.
I think I have some old vegetables I harvested from a village...

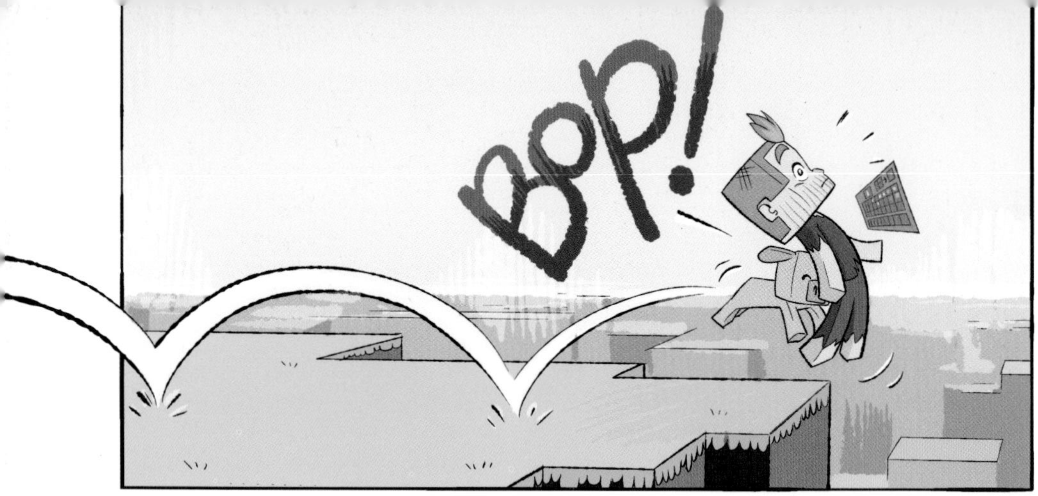
BOP!

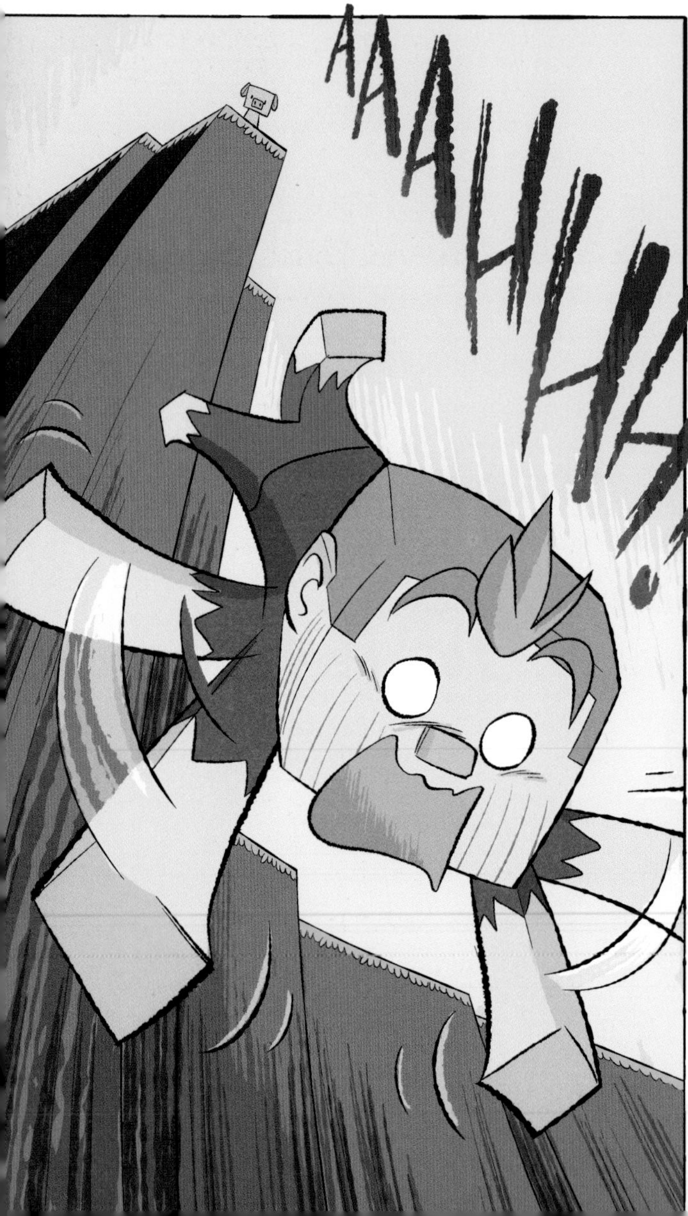
AAAHHHH!!

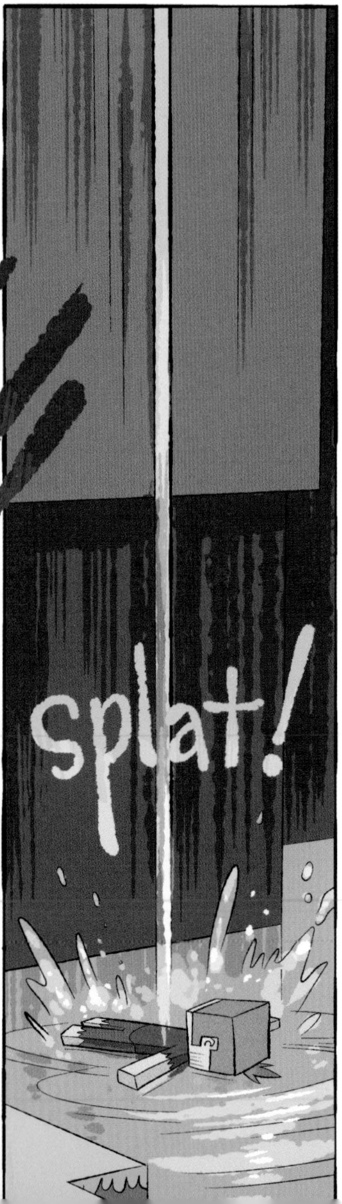
splat!

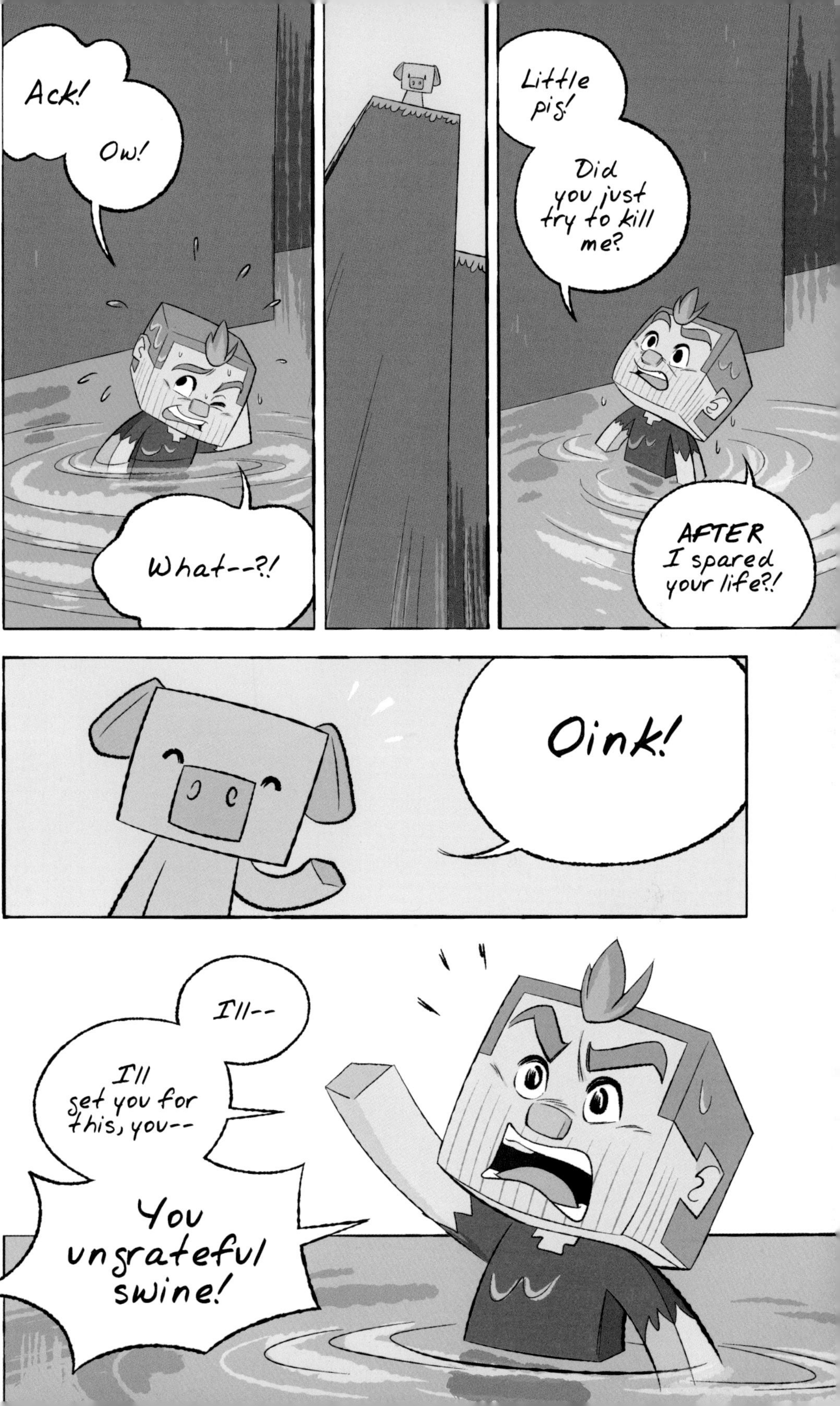
Ack!
Ow!
What--?!
Little pig!
Did you just try to kill me?
AFTER I spared your life?!
Oink!
I'll--
I'll get you for this, you--
You ungrateful swine!

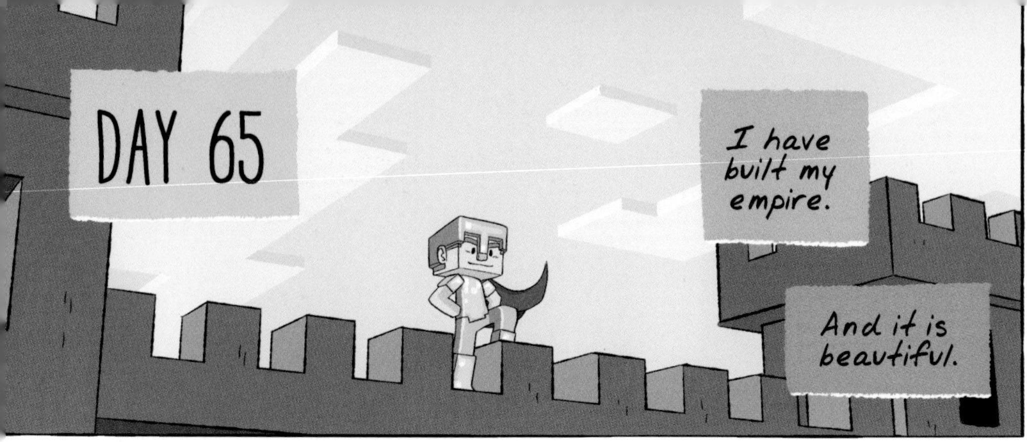
DAY 65
I have built my empire.
And it is beautiful.

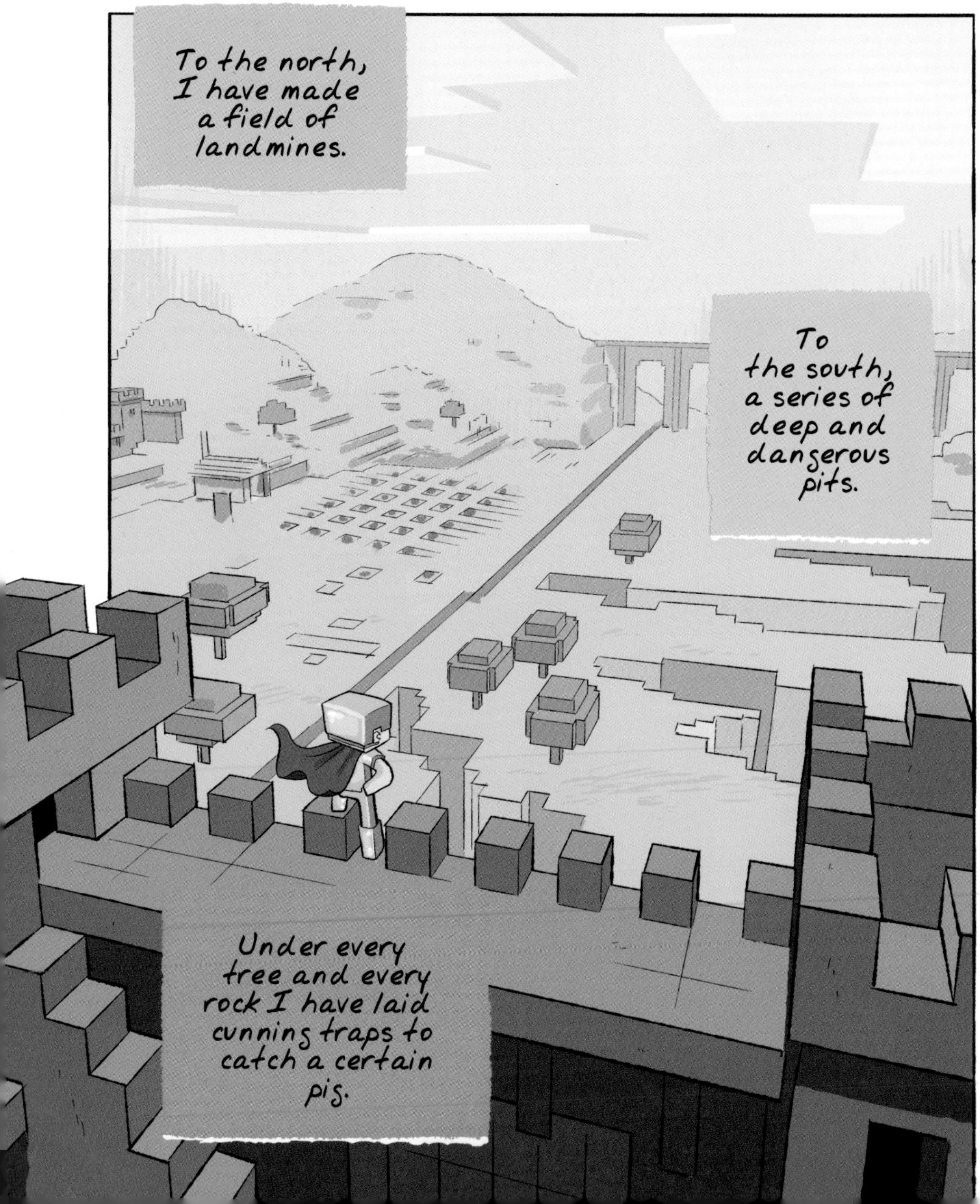
To the north, I have made a field of landmines.
To the south, a series of deep and dangerous pits.
Under every tree and every rock I have laid cunning traps to catch a certain pig.

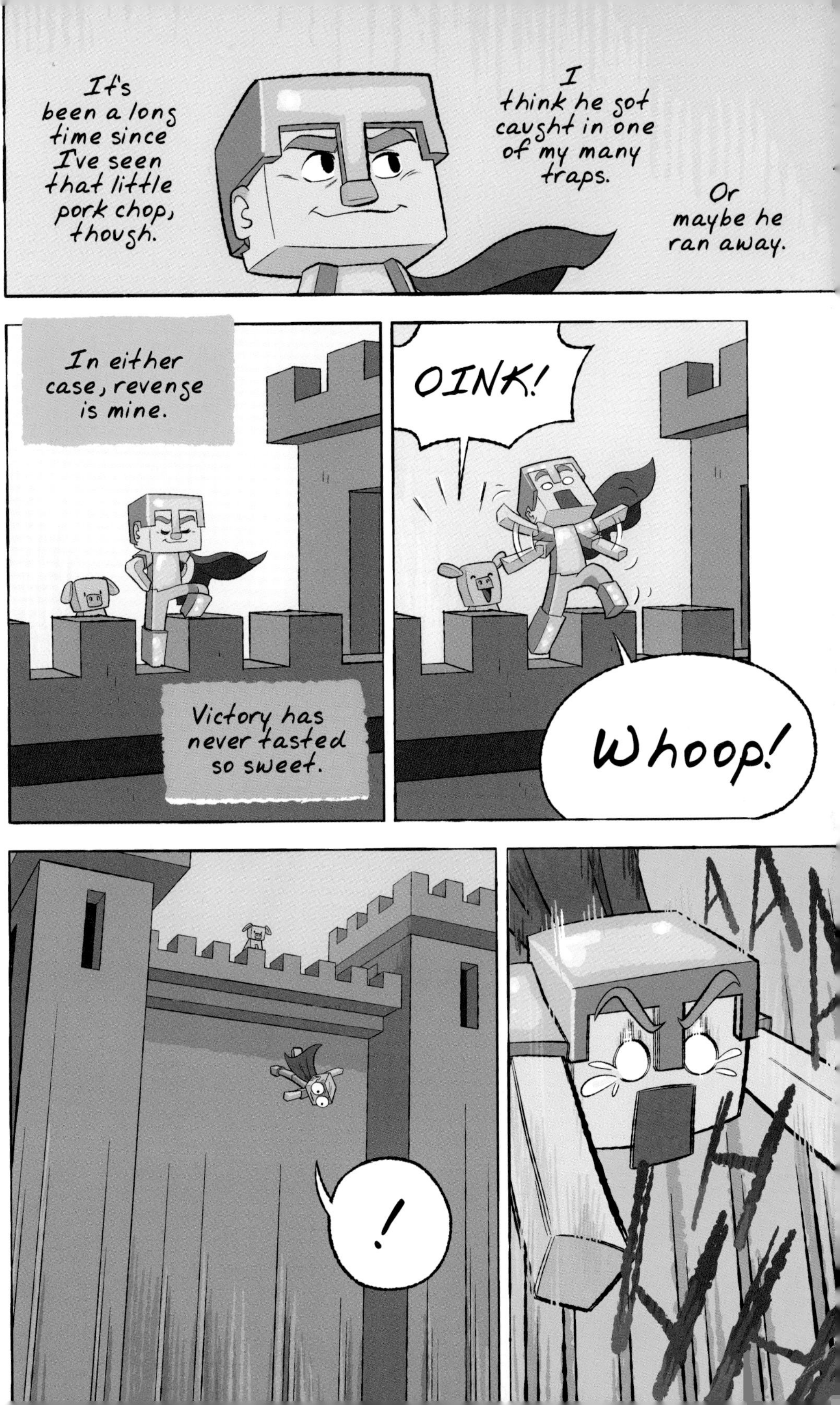
It's been a long time since I've seen that little pork chop, though.
I think he got caught in one of my many traps.
Or maybe he ran away.
In either case, revenge is mine.
Victory has never tasted so sweet.
OINK!
Whoop!
!

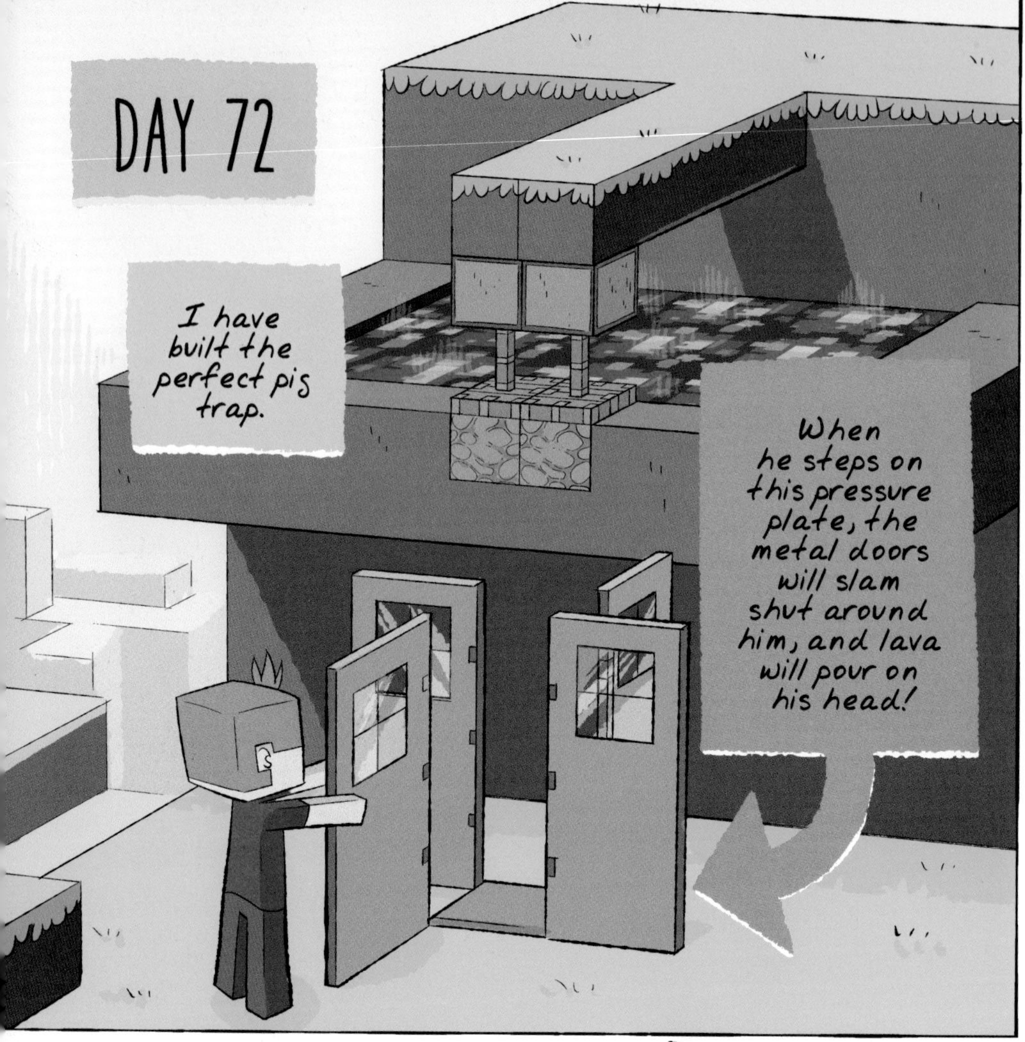
DAY 72
I have built the perfect pig trap.
When he steps on this pressure plate, the metal doors will slam shut around him, and lava will pour on his head!
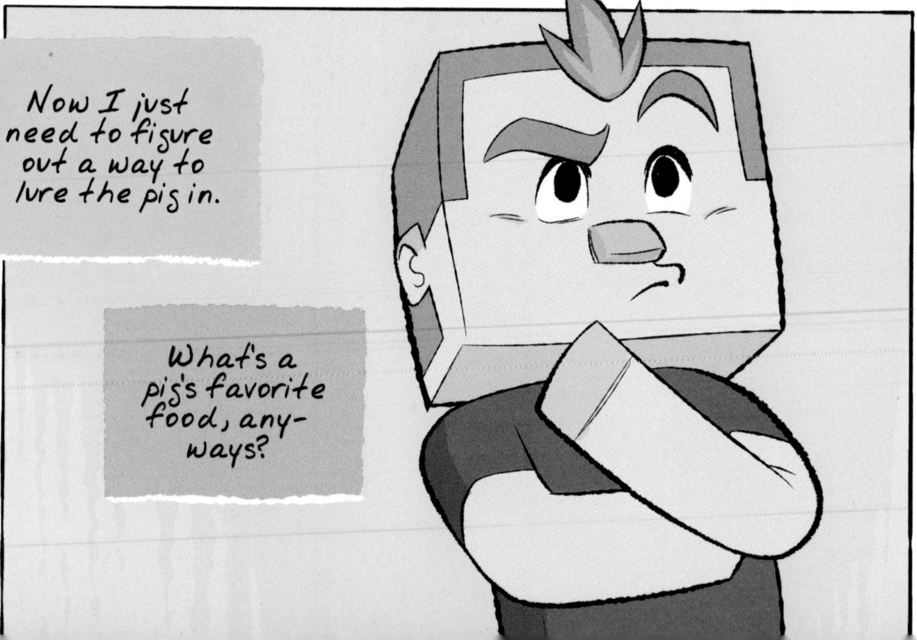
Now I just need to figure out a way to lure the pig in.
What's a pig's favorite food, any-ways?

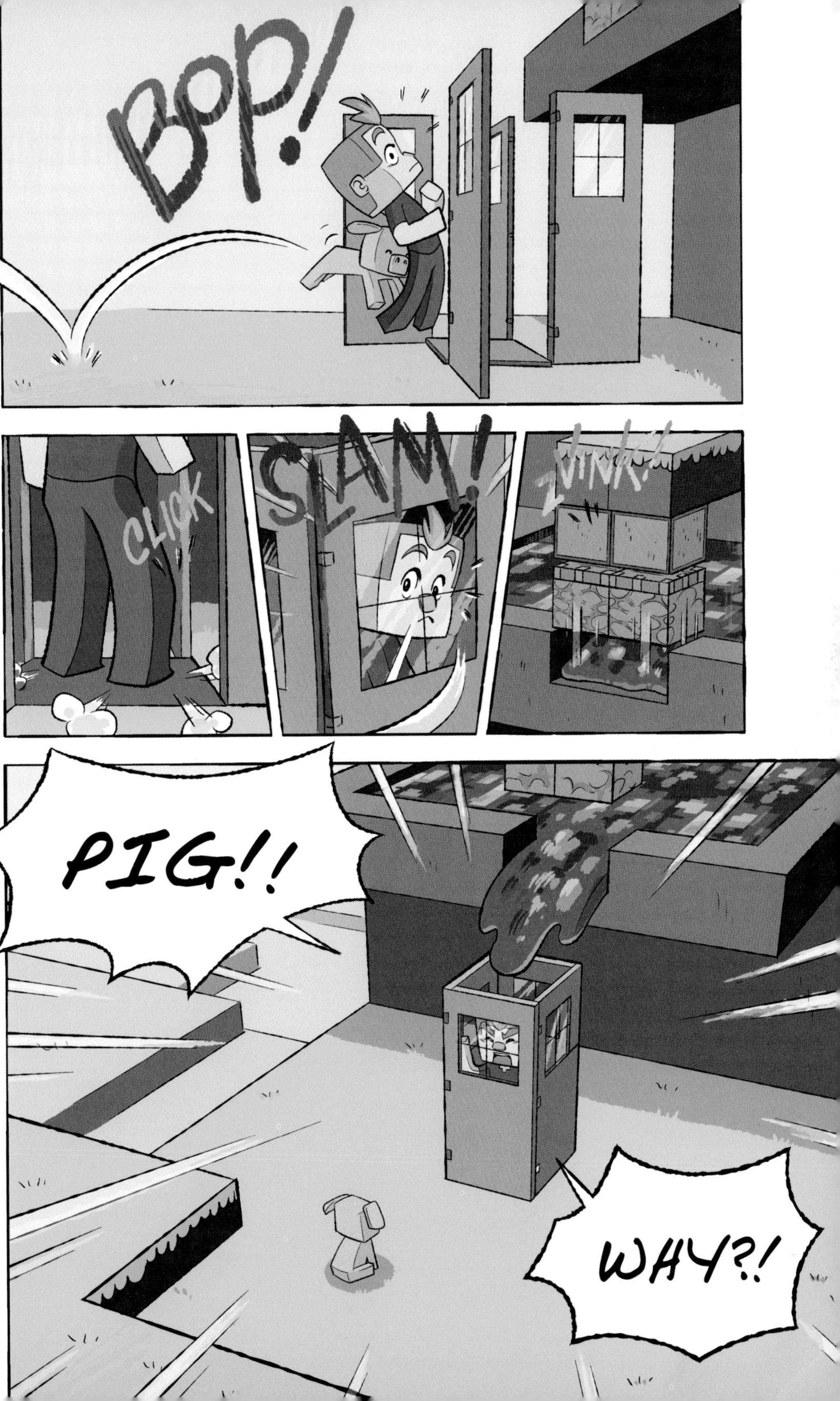
BOP!
CLICK
SLAM!
ZVINK!!
PIG!!
WHY?!

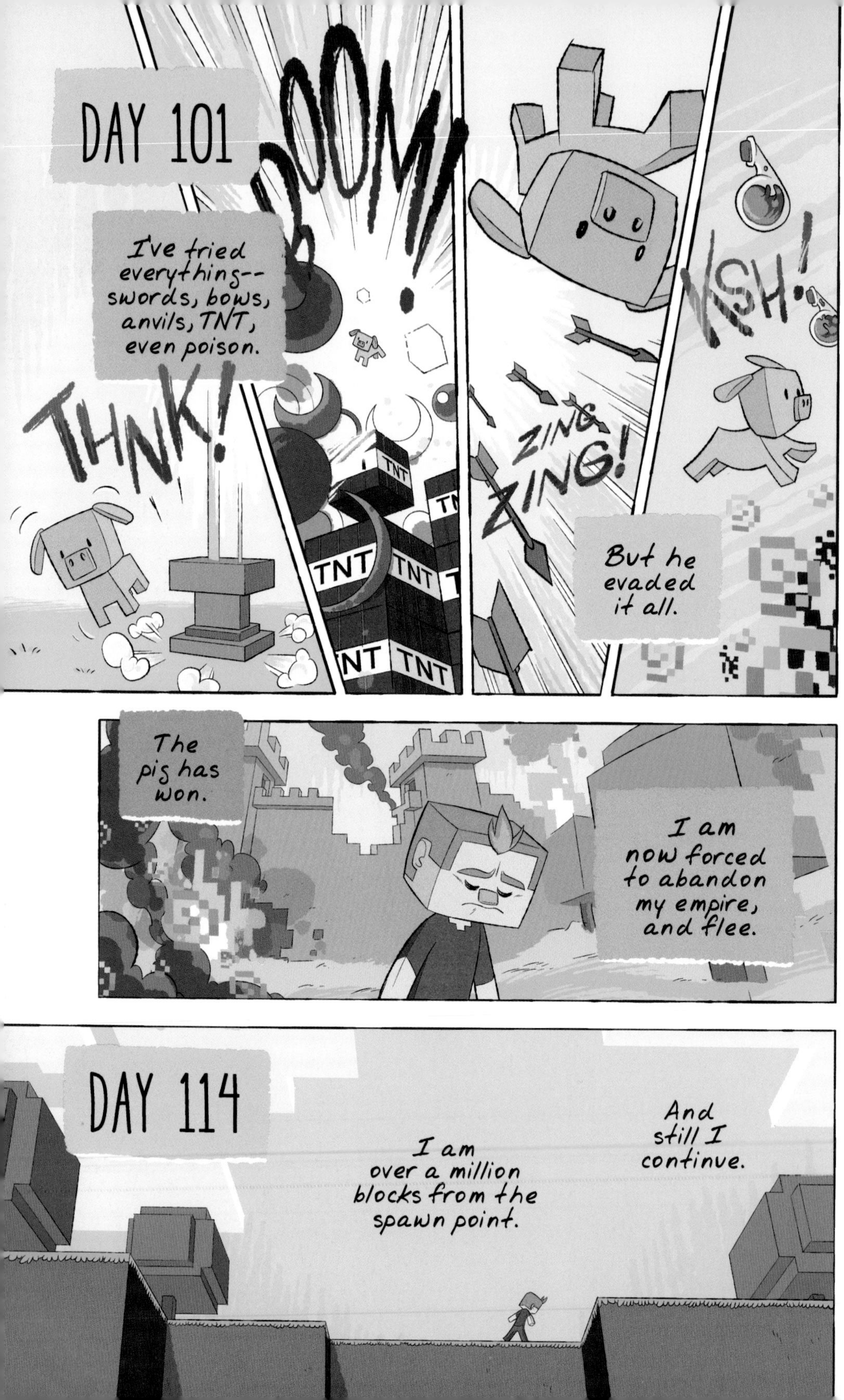
DAY 101
I've tried everything--swords, bows, anvils, TNT, even poison.
THNK!
BOOM!
ZING ZING!
But he evaded it all.
The pig has won.
I am now forced to abandon my empire, and flee.
DAY 114
I am over a million blocks from the spawn point.
And still I continue.

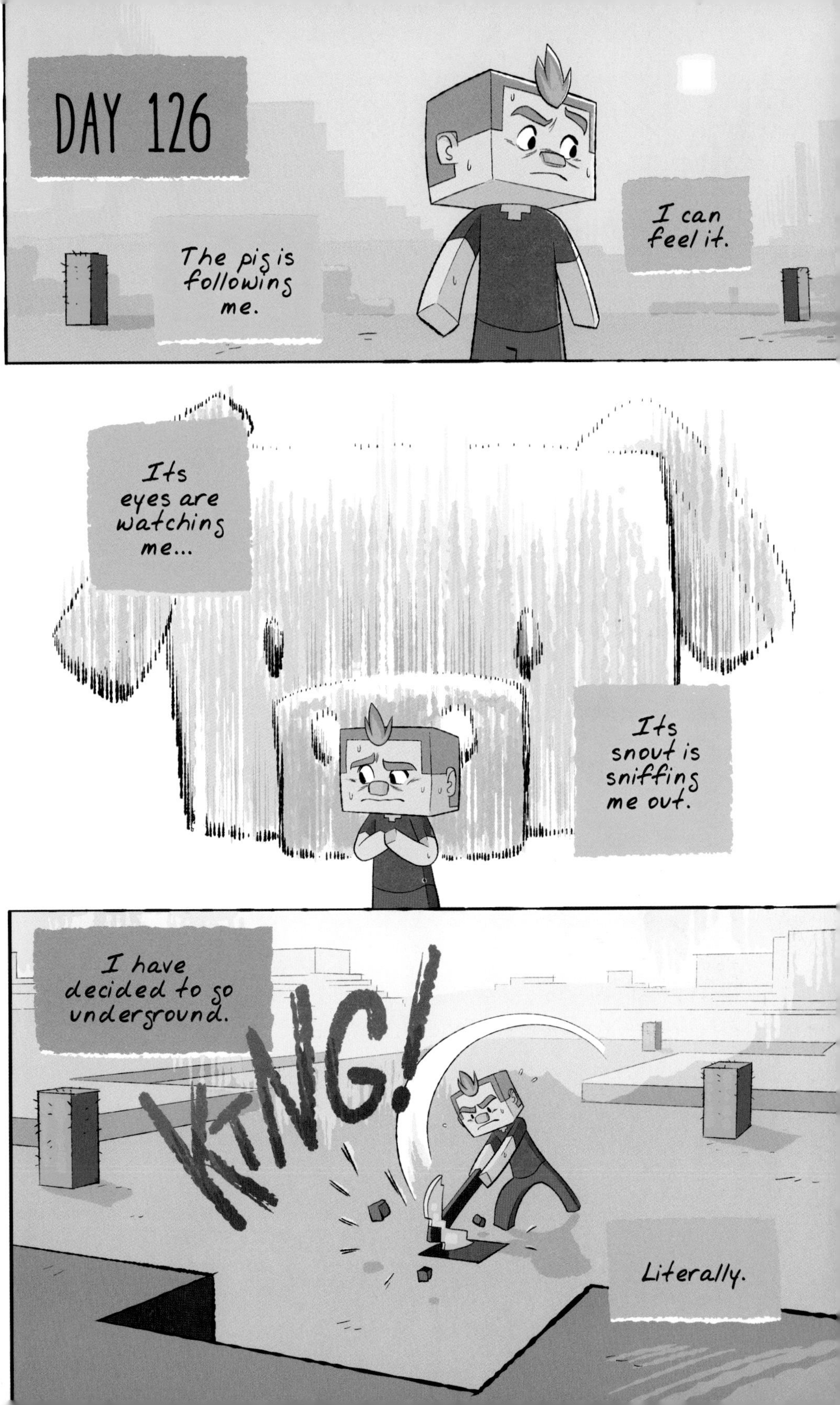
DAY 126
The pig is following me.
I can feel it.
Its eyes are watching me...
Its snout is sniffing me out.
I have decided to go underground.
KTING!
Literally.

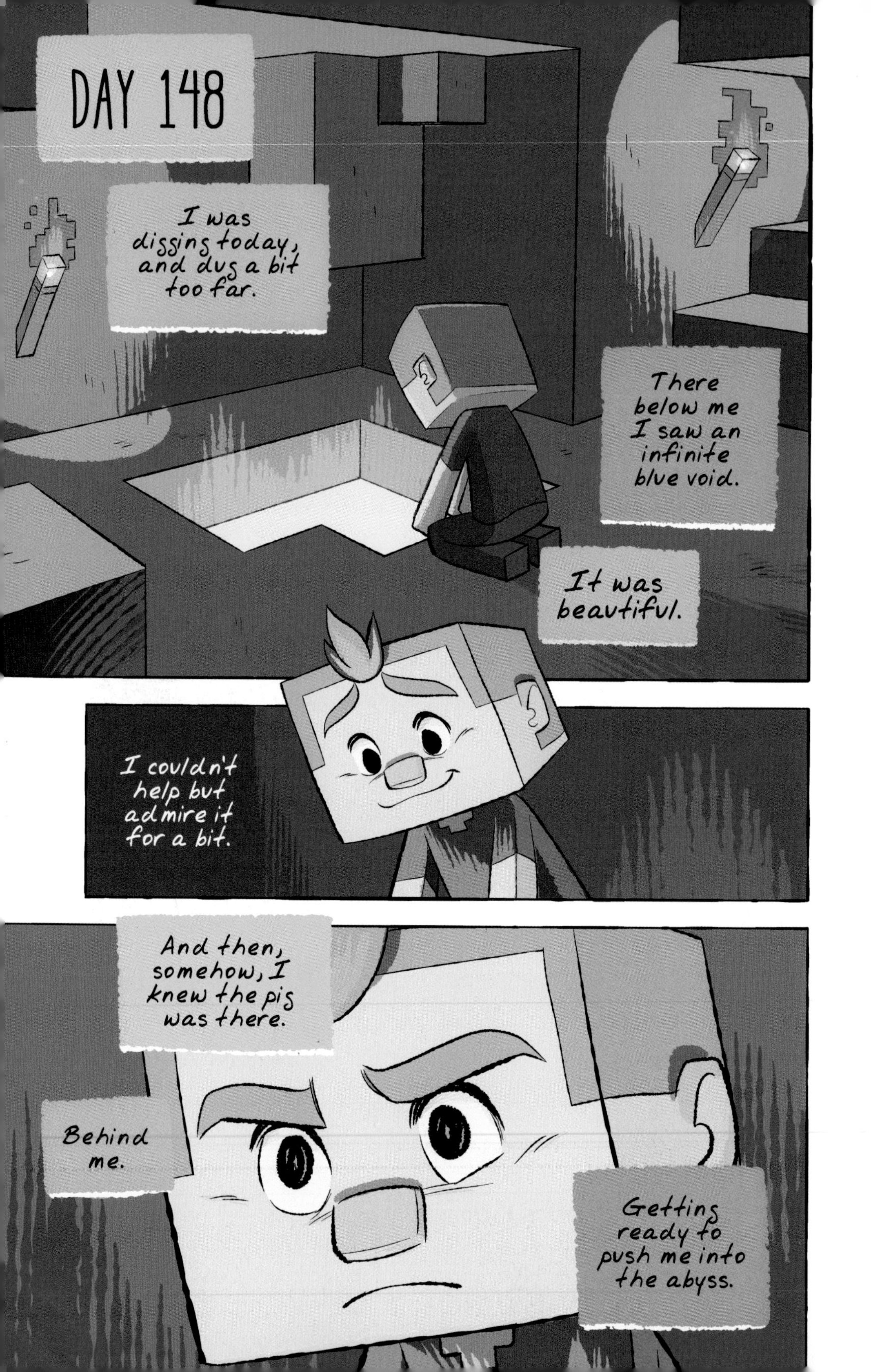
DAY 148
I was digging today, and dug a bit too far.
There below me I saw an infinite blue void.
It was beautiful.
I couldn't help but admire it for a bit.
And then, somehow, I knew the pig was there.
Behind me.
Getting ready to push me into the abyss.

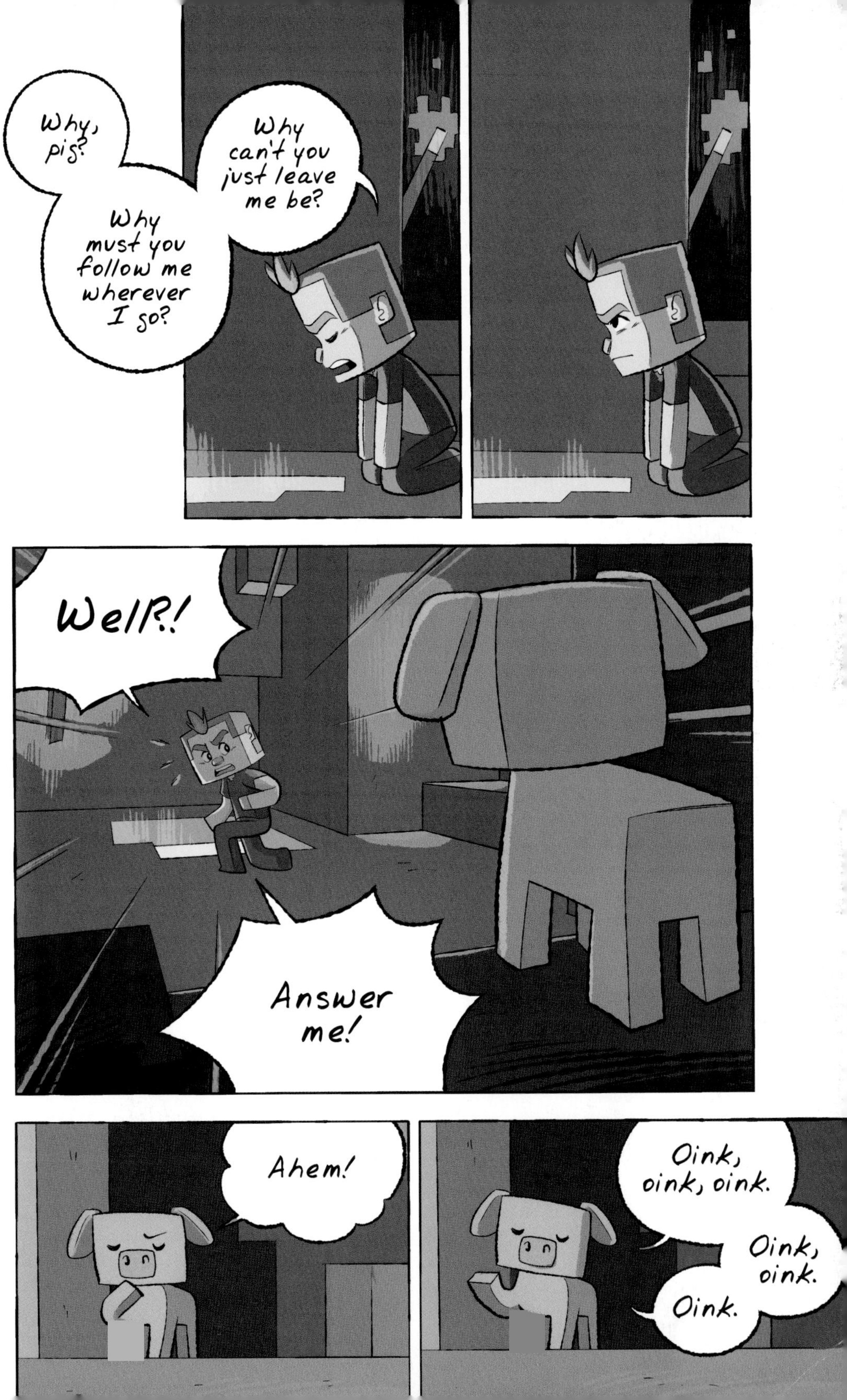
Why, pig?
Why must you follow me wherever I go?
Why can't you just leave me be?
Well?!
Answer me!
Ahem!
Oink, oink, oink.
Oink, oink.
Oink.

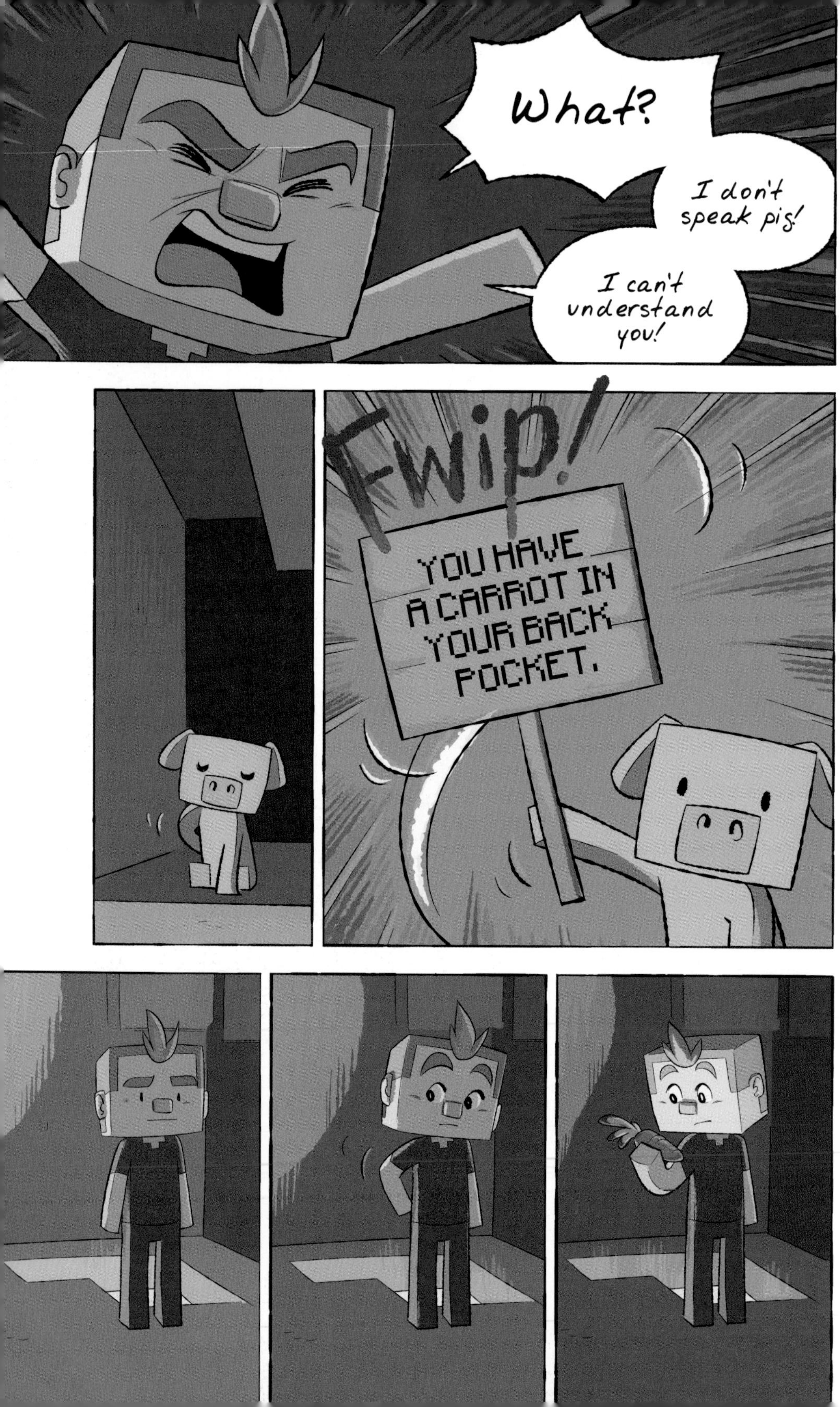

What?
I don't speak pig!
I can't understand you!
FWIP!
YOU HAVE A CARROT IN YOUR BACK POCKET.

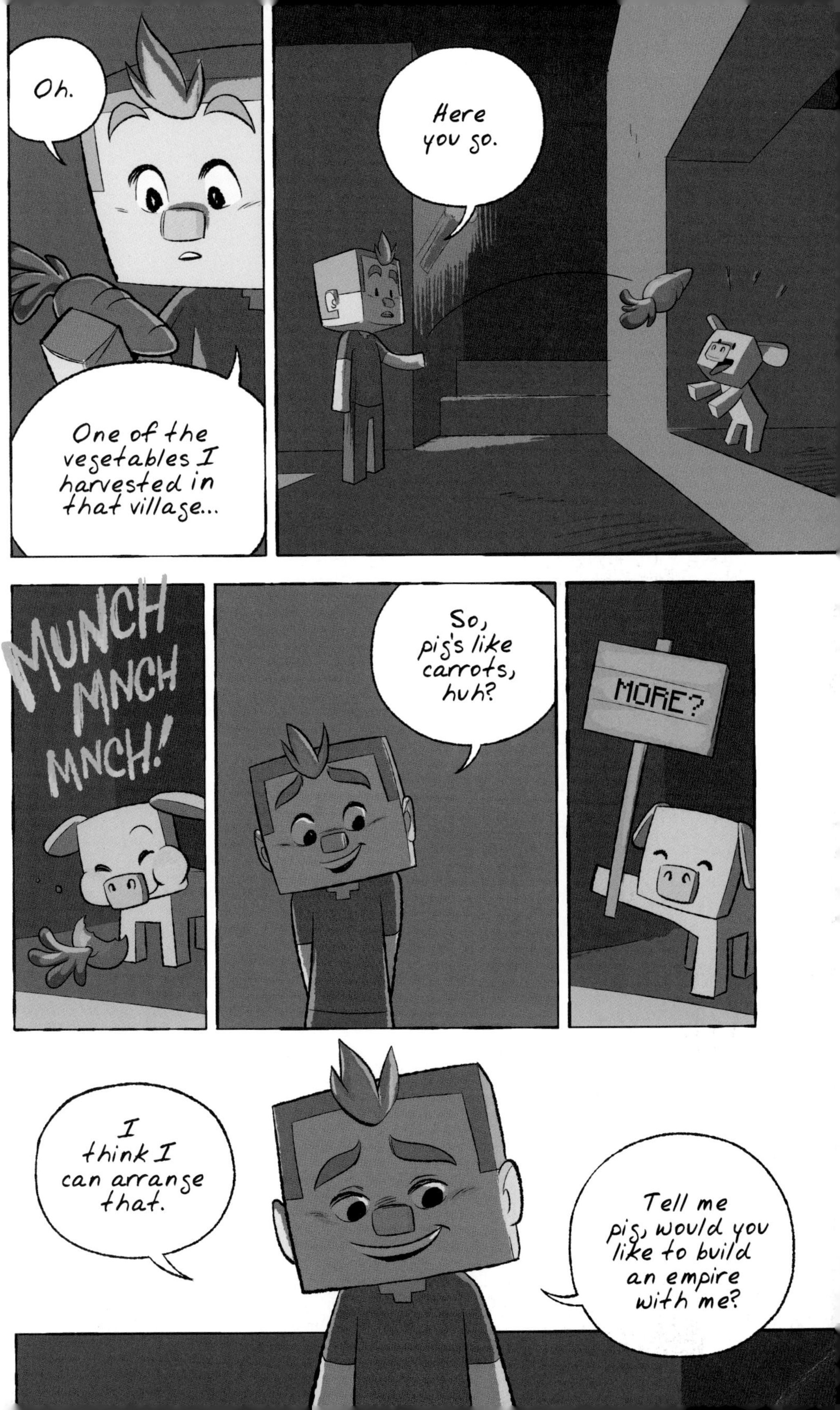
Oh.
One of the vegetables I harvested in that village...
Here you go.
MUNCH MNCH MNCH!
So, pig's like carrots, huh?
MORE?
I think I can arrange that.
Tell me pig, would you like to build an empire with me?

DAY 216

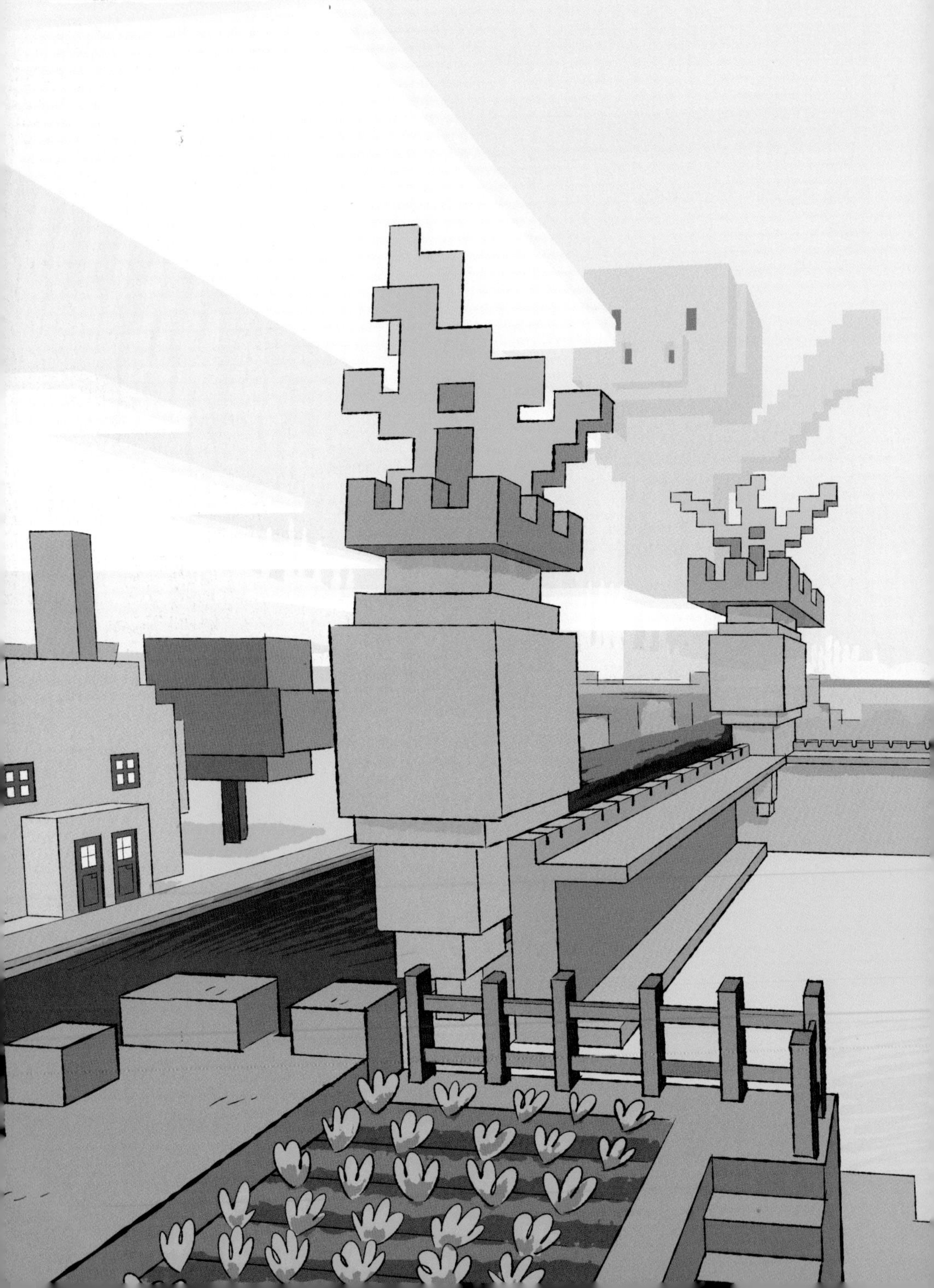

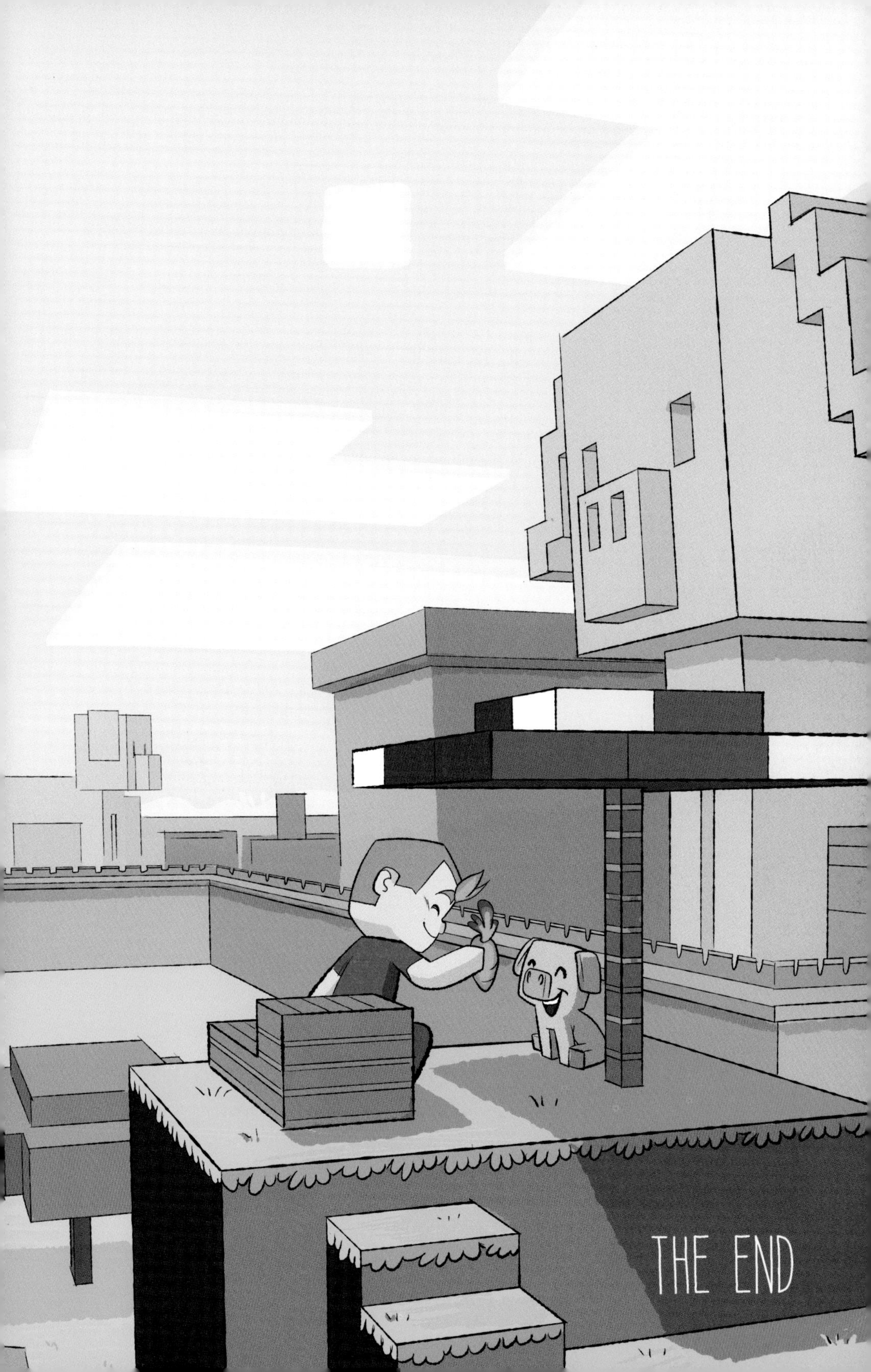
THE END

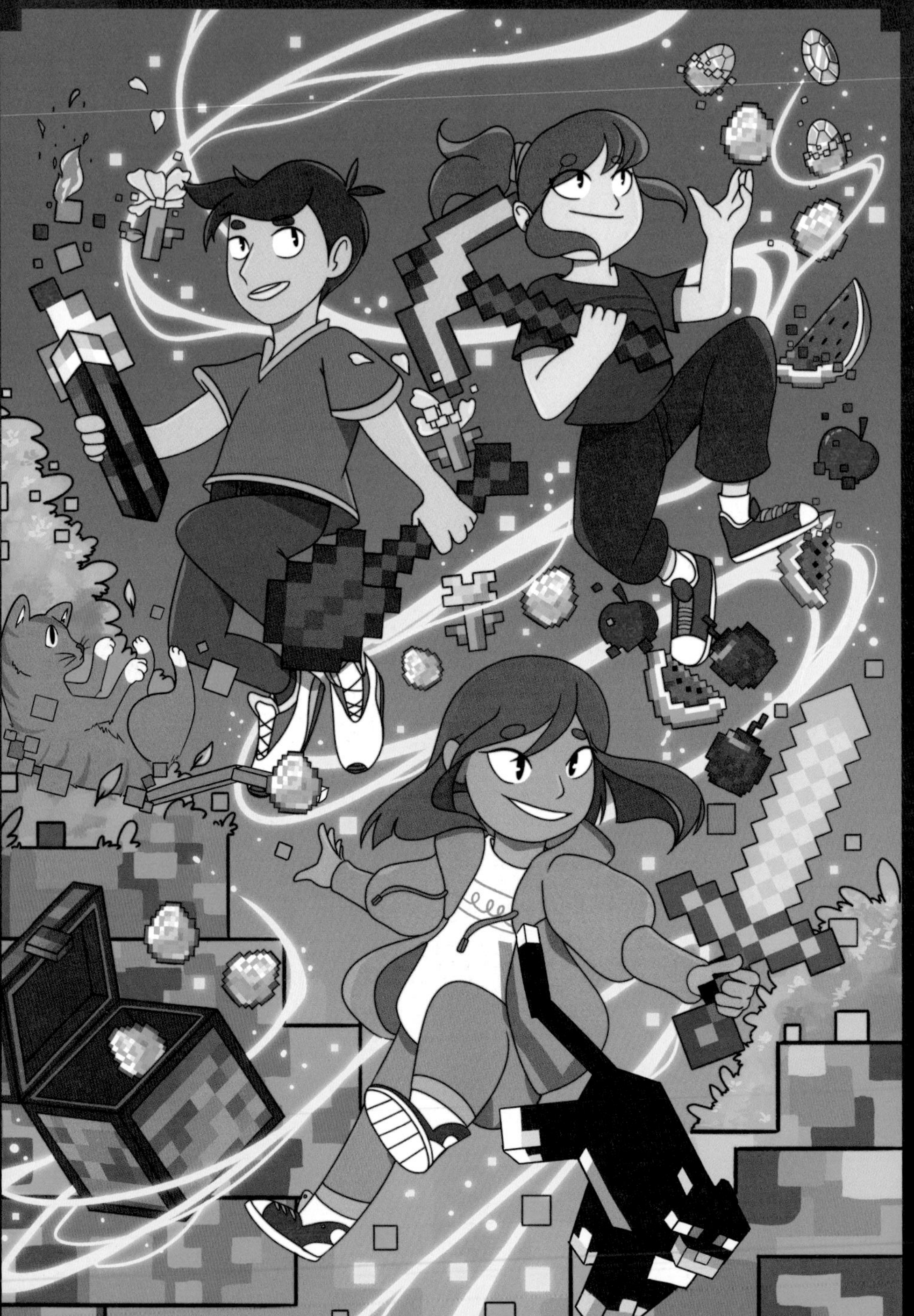

ILLUSTRATION BY

KAT HALL

A STRANGE SHORE

STORY BY
IAN FLYNN

ART BY
JENN ST-ONGE

COLORS BY
TRIONA FARRELL

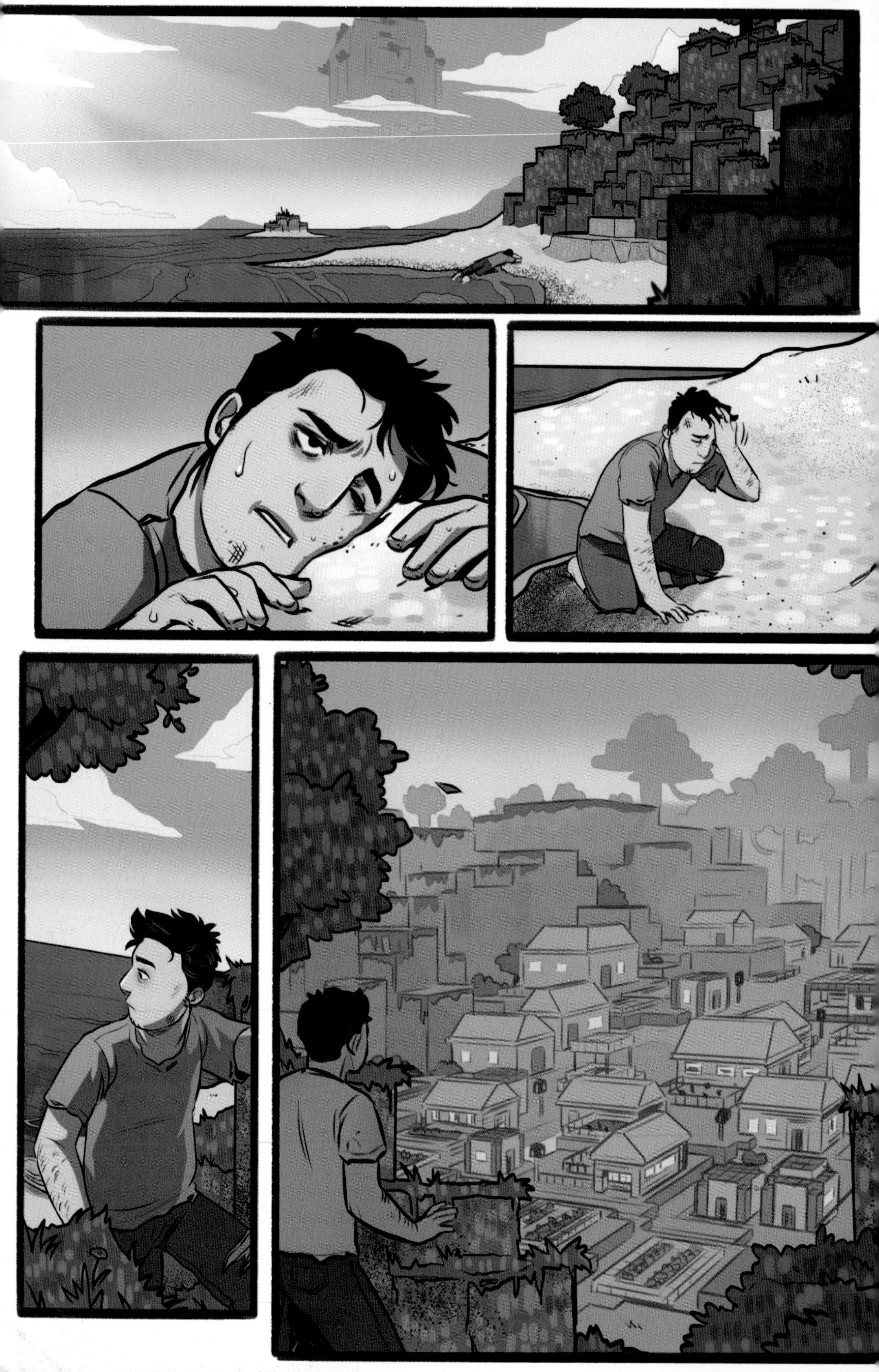

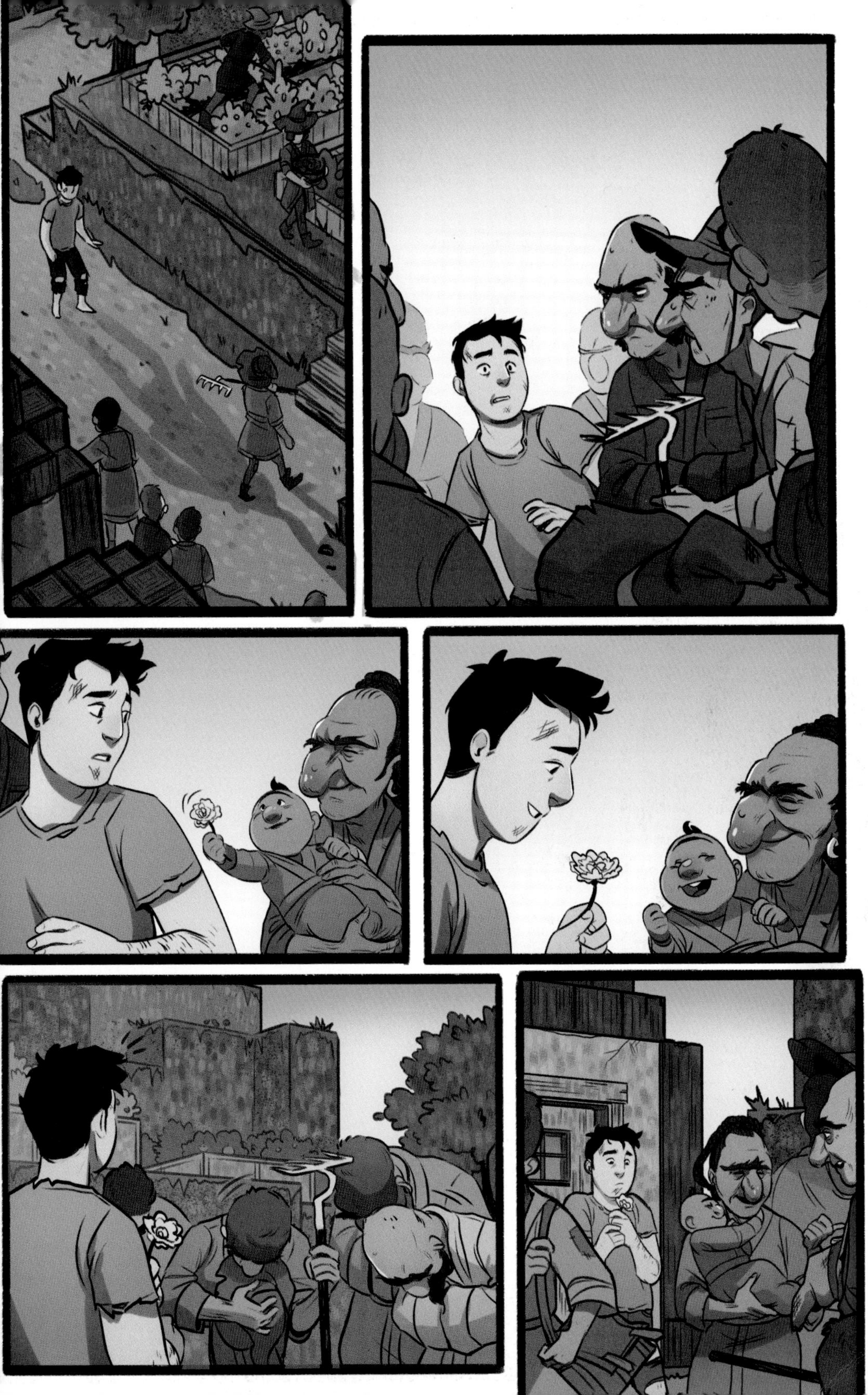

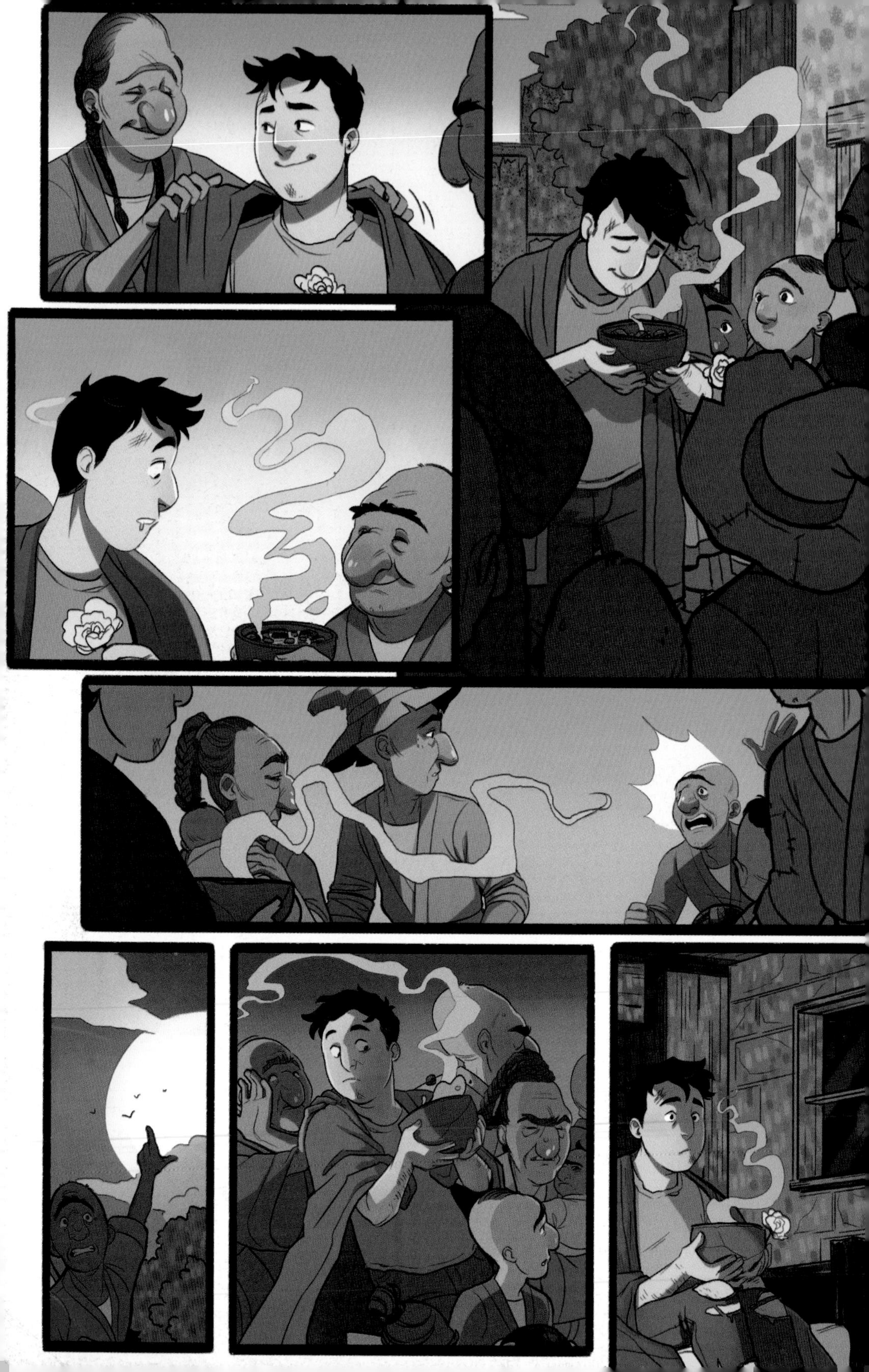

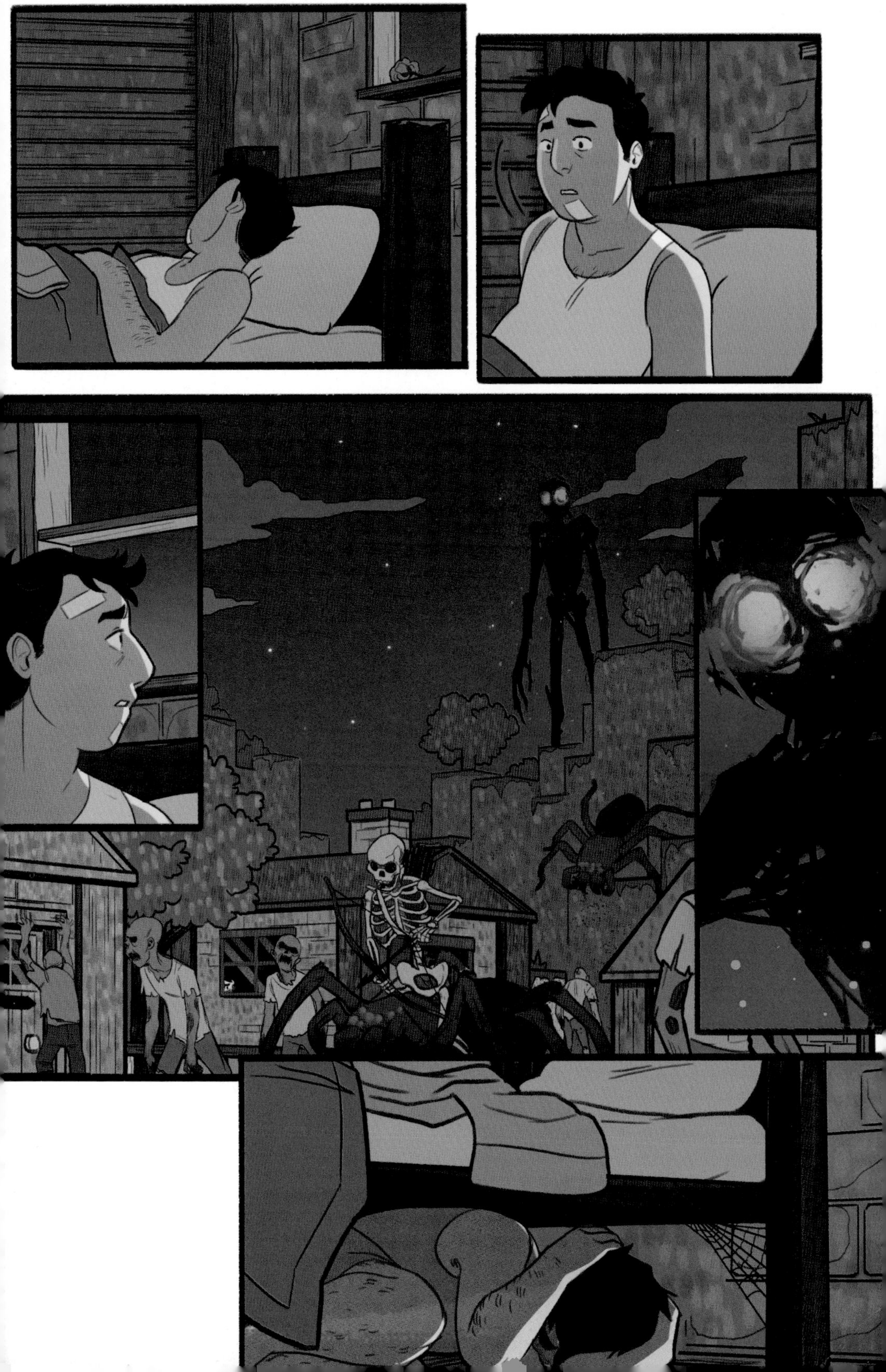

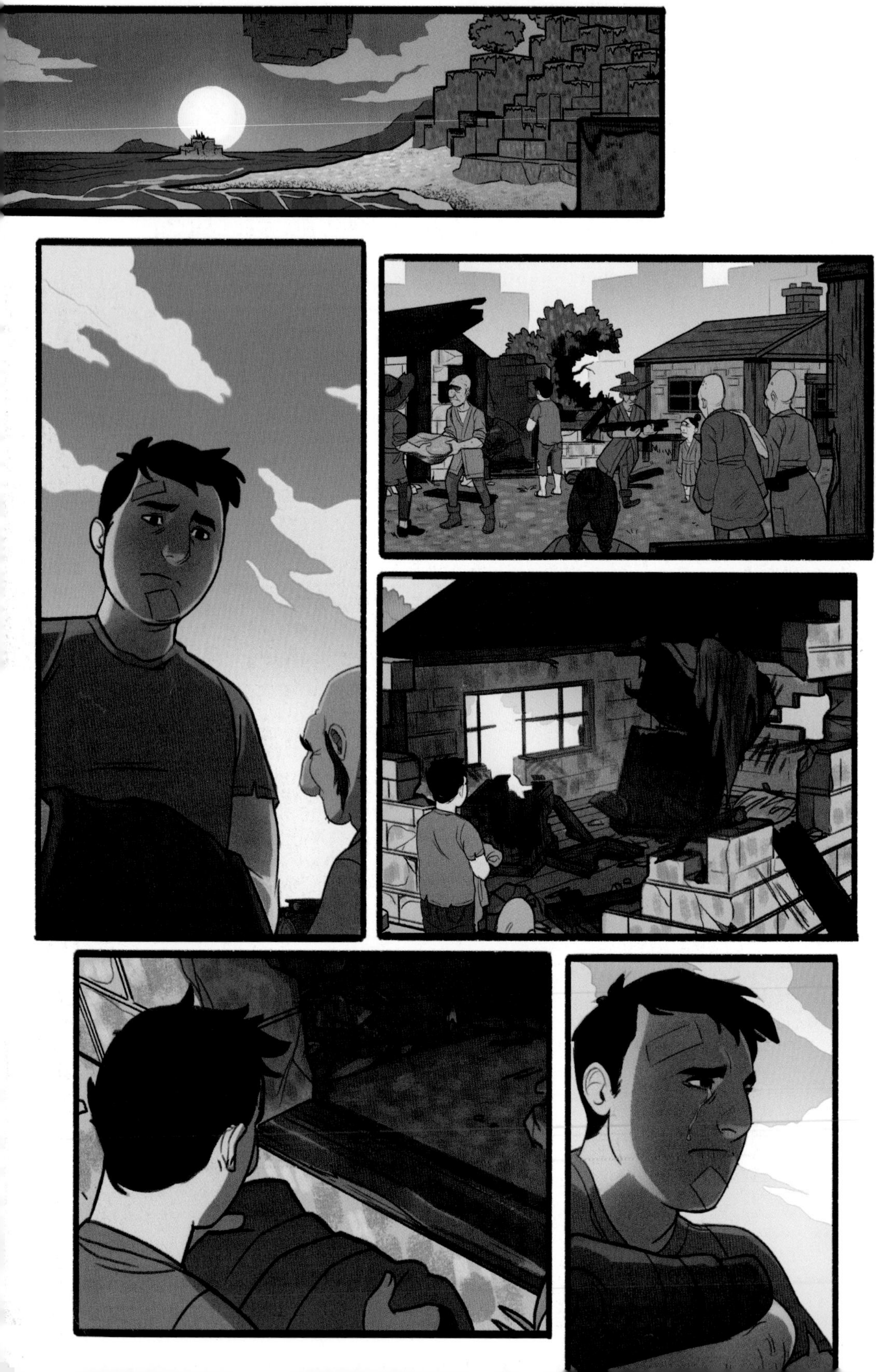

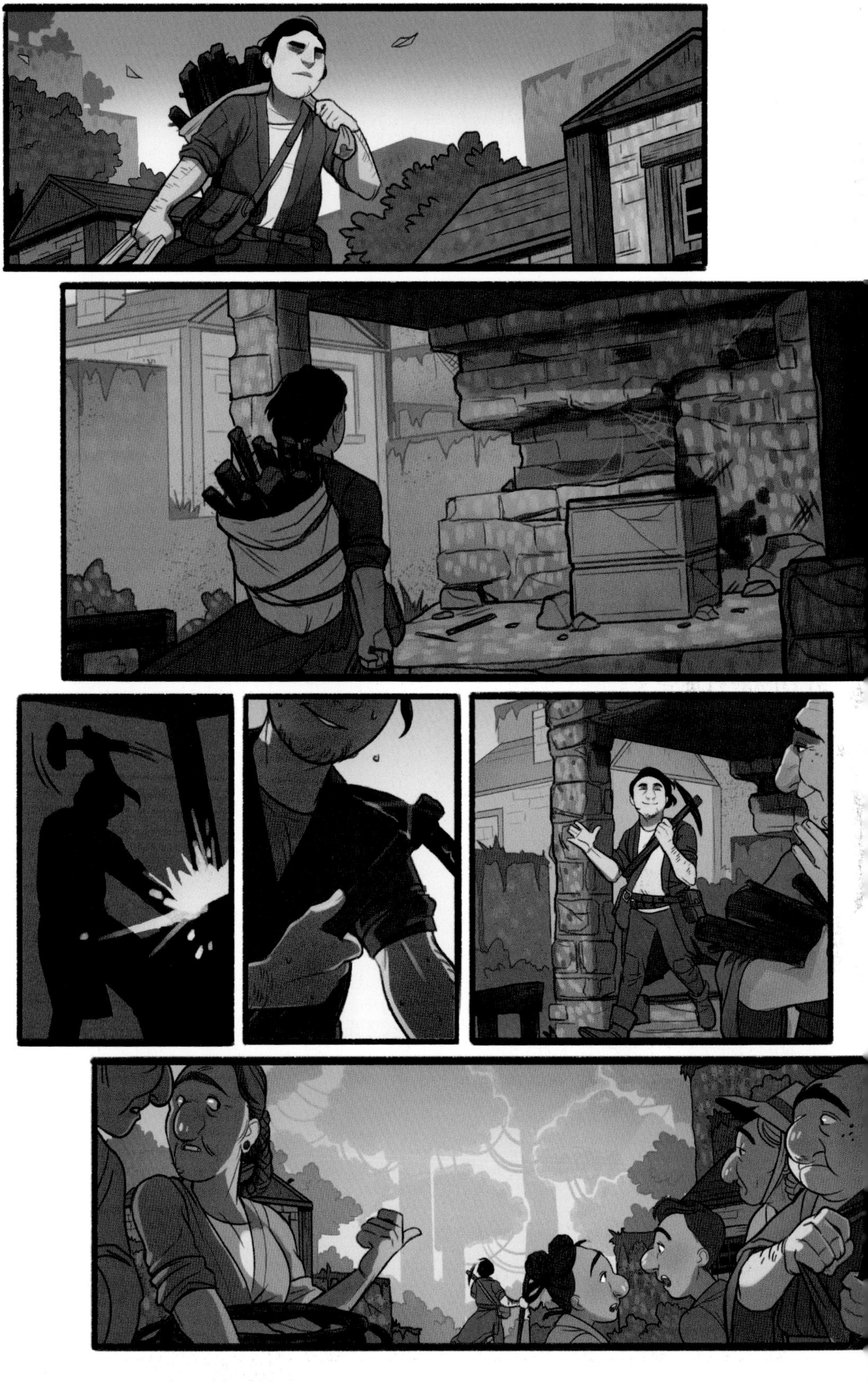

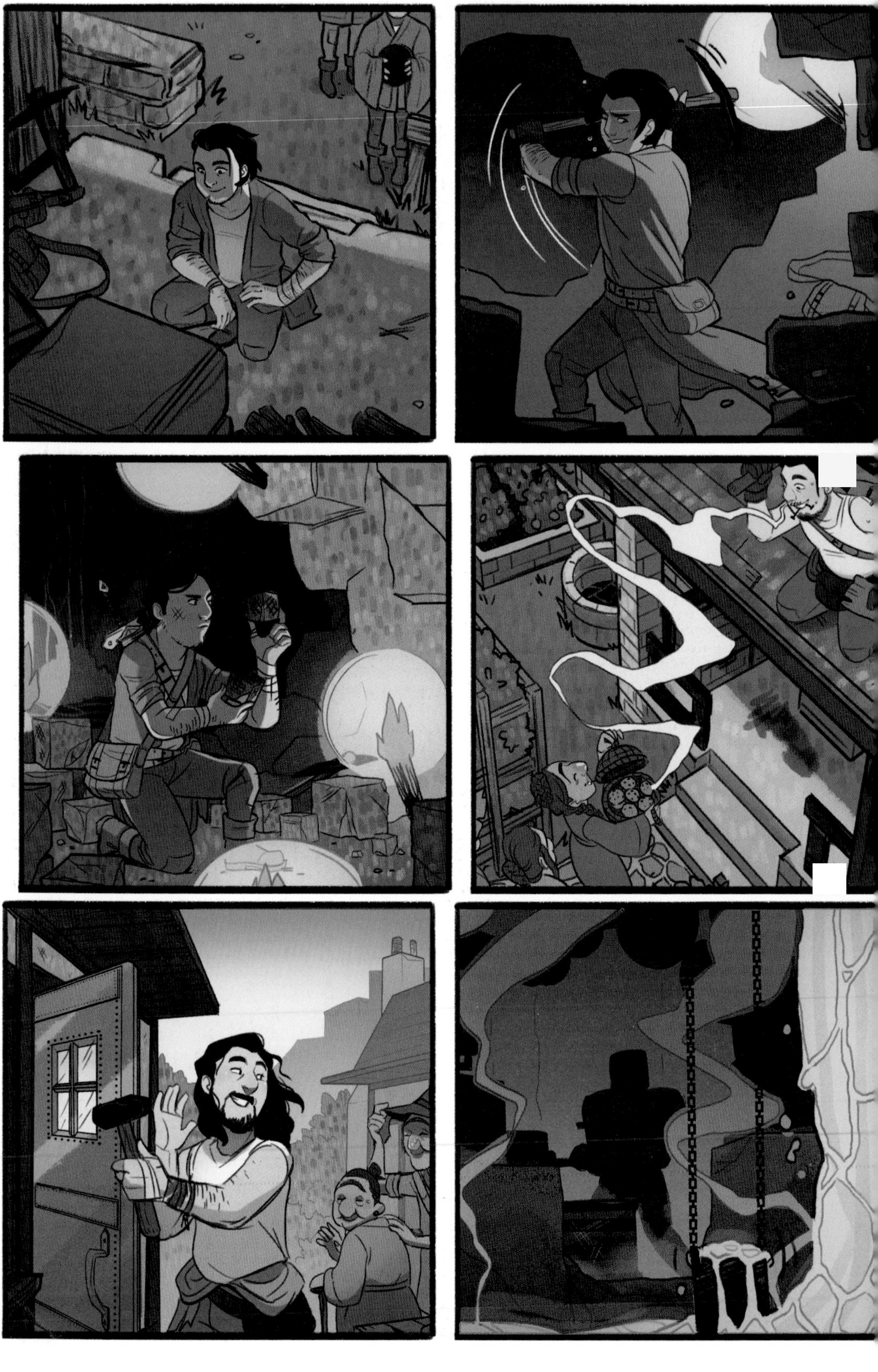

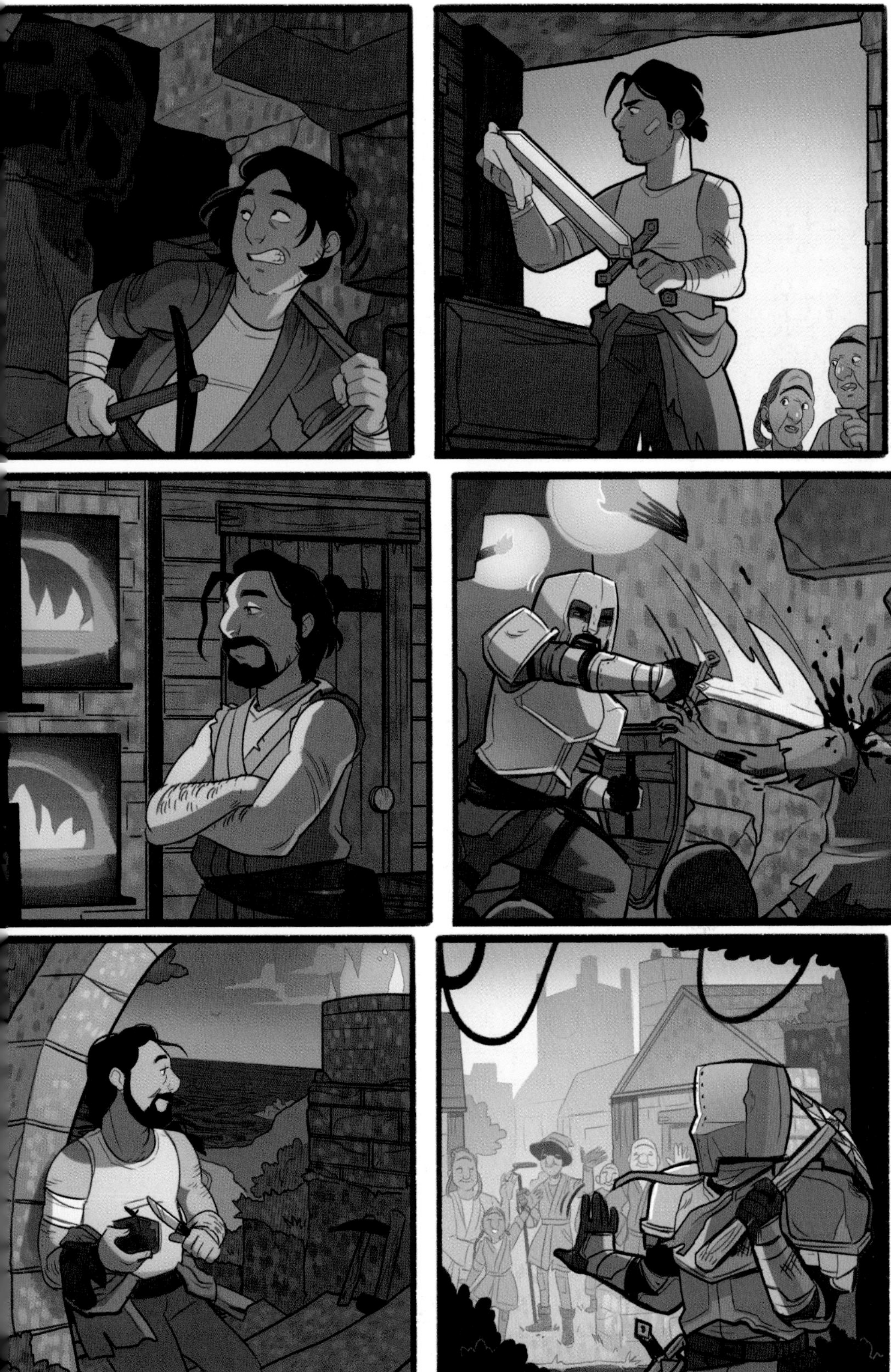

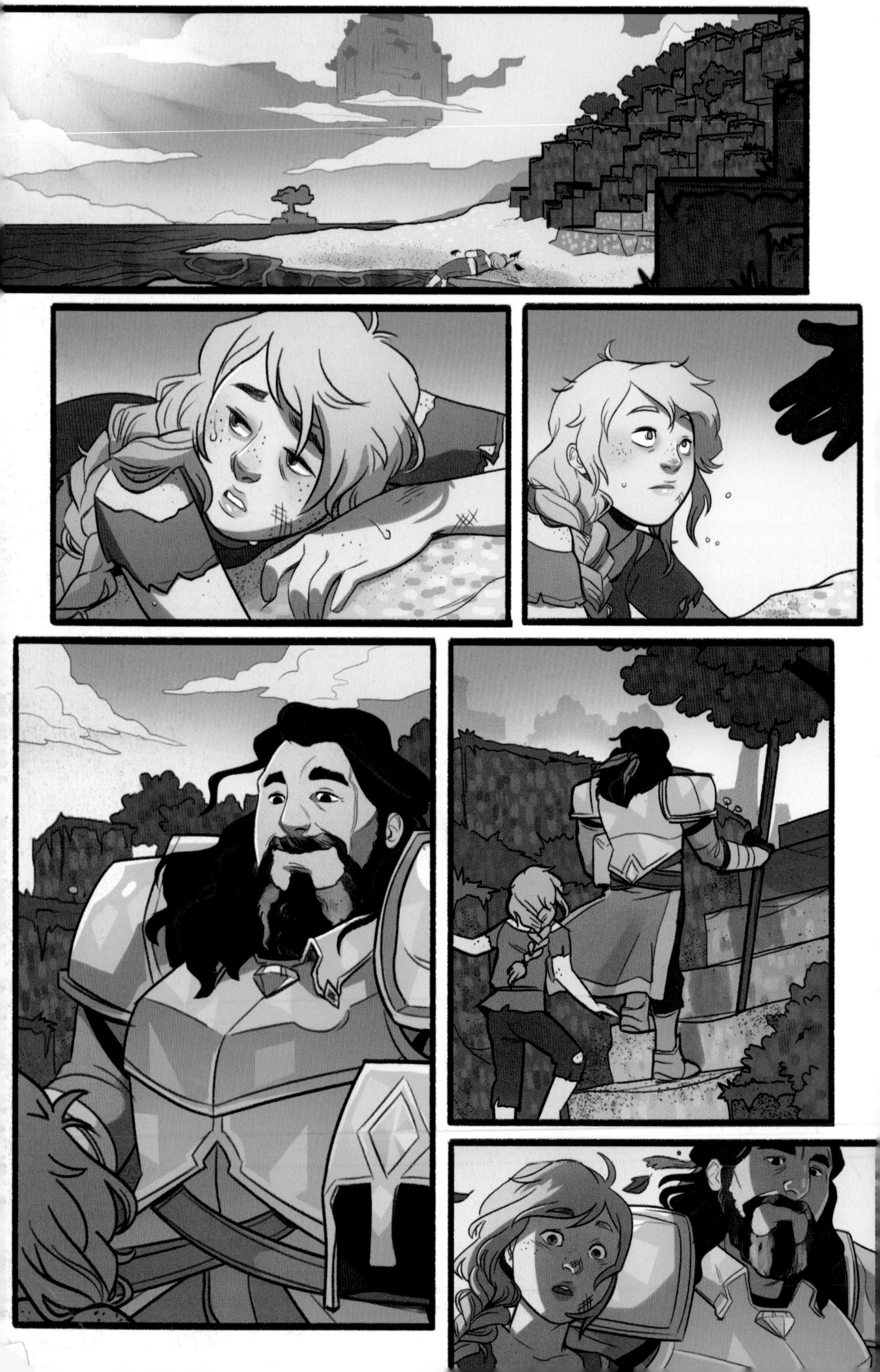

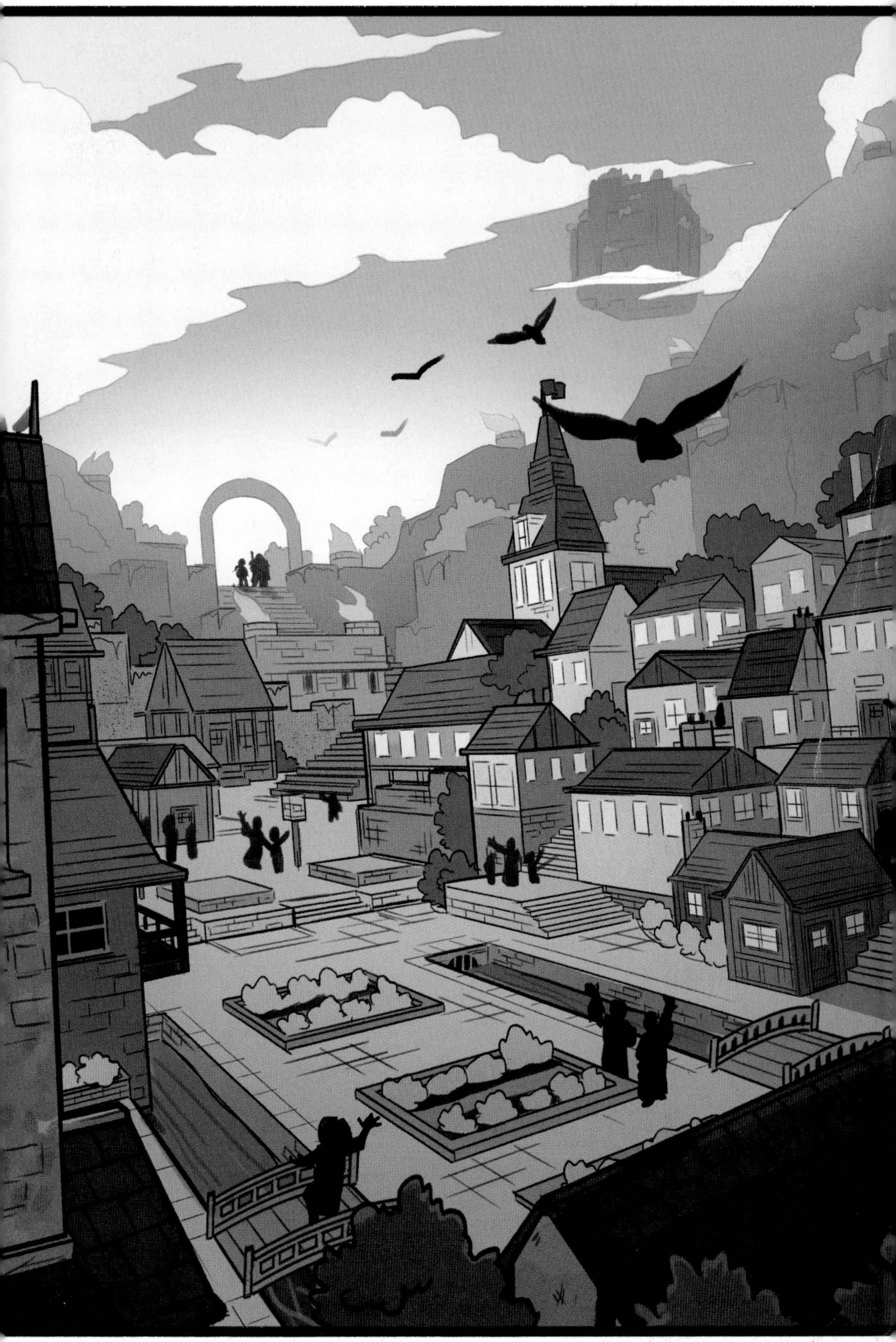

AVAILABLE NOW...

MINECRAFT

SFÉ R. MONSTER, SARAH GRALEY, JOHN J. HILL

Tyler is your everyday kid whose life is changed when his family has to move from the town he's always known. Thankfully, Tyler has a strong group of friends forever linked in the world of Minecraft! Tyler, along with his friends Evan, Candace, Tobi, and Grace have been going on countless adventures together across the expanses of the Overworld and are in need of a new challenge. They decide to go on the Ultimate Quest—to travel to the End and face off against the ender dragon!

Volume 1 · ISBN 978-1-50670-834-8	$10.99
Volume 2 · ISBN 978-1-50670-836-2	$10.99

MINECRAFT: STORIES FROM THE OVERWORLD

From blocks to panels, Minecraft explorations are crafted into comics in this anthology collection!

With tales of witch and pillager rivals finding common ground, a heartless griefer who bit off more than they could chew, and valiant heroes new (or not!) to the Overworld, this anthology tells tales that span the world of Minecraft. Featuring stories from star writers and exciting artists, this collection brings together stories from all realms, leaving no block unturned!

ISBN 978-1-50670-833-1	$14.99

MINECRAFT: WITHER WITHOUT YOU
KRISTEN GUDSNUK

Jump into the Overworld with the first adventure of a three-part series from the world's best-selling videogame Minecraft!

Cahira and Orion are twin monster hunters under the tutelage of Senan the Thorough. After an intense battle with an enchanted wither, their mentor is eaten and the twins are now alone! The two hunters go on a mission to get their mentor back, and meet an unlikely ally along the way!

Volume 1 · ISBN 978-1-50670-835-5	$10.99
Volume 2 · ISBN 978-1-50671-886-6	$10.99

AVAILABLE AT YOUR LOCAL COMICS SHOP OR BOOKSTORE!
To find a comics shop in your area, visit comicshoplocator.com.
For more information or to order direct visit DarkHorse.com

™ & © 2020, 2021 Mojang AB. All rights reserved. Minecraft, the Minecraft logo and the Mojang Studios logo are trademarks of the Microsoft group of companies. Dark Horse Books® and the Dark Horse logo are registered trademarks of Dark Horse Comics LLC. All rights reserved.